COPING
IN
A Single-
Parent
Home

Bill R. Wagonseller,

Lynne C. Ruegamer and

Marie C. Harrington

THE ROSEN PUBLISHING GROUP, INC./NEW YORK

Published in 1992, 1995, 1998 by The Rosen Publishing Group, Inc.
29 East 21st Street, New York, NY 10010

Copyright 1992, 1995, 1998 by Bill R. Wagonseller, Lynne C.
Ruegamer, Marie C. Harrington

Revised Edition 1997

Wagonseller, Bill R.
    Coping in a single-parent home / Bill R. Wagonseller,
Lynne C. Ruegamer, and Marie C. Harrington.—rev. ed.
    p. cm.
    Includes bibliographical references and index.
    Summary: Discusses coping with the problems of living in a
single-parent home.
    ISBN 0-8239-2625-7
    1. Children of single parents—United States—Juvenile
literature. [1. Single-parent family. 2. Family problems.
3. family life.] I. Ruegamer, Lynne C. II. Harrington, Marie.
III. Title.
HQ777.4.W34   1992
306.85'6—dc20
                                                    91-41178
                                                    CIP
                                                    AC

Manufactured in the United States of America

ABOUT THE AUTHORS ◇

D r. Bill R. Wagonseller is a professor of Special Education at the University of Nevada, Las Vegas. He serves as director of UNLV's Parent/Family Wellness Center and coordinator of the Emotional Disturbance Teacher Training program. For the past twenty-five years he has been developing parent-training materials, which are used in churches, schools, and agencies and by families throughout the world.

Dr. Wagonseller began his professional teaching career in the Wichita public schools as a teacher/administrator of the Lake Afton Boy's Ranch, a detention center for delinquent boys. He has earned numerous awards for teaching excellence, including UNLV's Distinguished Faculty Award in 1982 and Distinguished Teaching Award in 1983 and the Lilly Fong Distinguished Teacher Award in 1986–87. He also received the Exemplar Community Service Award from the University of Notre Dame. Dr. Wagonseller has served as a consultant to many school districts and agencies and has received a recognition award from the Las Vegas chapter of Phi Delta Kappa for leadership in education. He has published numerous professional papers and scholarly articles, is coauthor of *TIP: Teaching Involved Parenting*, *The Art of Parenting*, and *You and Your Child*, and also is program developer of the Practical Parenting (15 part) Video Series. The series covers most of the family lifestyles in today's society, including teenage pregnancy, single parenting, and blended families.

Dr. Lynne C. Ruegamer is the Principal at Mountain Pine Elementary School at Ely, Nevada. She previously was a professor of Special Education and chairperson of that department at the University of Nevada, Las Vegas. She has served as coordinator of the Severe Mental Handicaps program and Generalist (Resource Room) teacher training program at UNLV.

She received her undergraduate degree in Political Science and History from the University of Montana. Graduate work was completed in Special Education, with emphasis on severe/profound handicaps and behavioral interventions. She has taught in institutions and public and private schools and worked as a consultant for school districts and state agencies.

While active in publishing, Dr. Ruegamer has received awards for excellence in teaching and served on numerous boards. Her areas of expertise include content related to "at-risk" children and youth, parent training, and single-parent families. Her two teenage sons provide "on-the-job" training in parenting and help keep materials relevant for today's families.

Marie C. Harrington is an elementary school teacher with the Clark County School District. She has also worked as a consultant for the Parent/Family Wellness Center at the University of Nevada, Las Vagas, researching parent education and facilitating correspondence between the center's director and parent interest groups.

She received her bachelor's degree in Psychology and Diversified Liberal Arts from the University of California, Los Angeles, and completed graduate work for Teacher Certification from UCLA's Teacher Education Lab. She recently had an article published in the Las Vegas-based *Kidz Magazine*, a parenting publication.

Acknowledgments

It would be impossible to name all the students, parents, and professionals who directly and indirectly contributed to this book. Special credit and thanks should be given to the students and professional staff at Bishop Gorman and Chaparral high schools and Cannon Junior High School. The students' input concerning problems and suggestions for coping were most valuable.

We give special thanks to our children for inspiring us and sharing their personal insights into parenting.

We would have never completed the book without the editing, typing, and retyping by Joyce Standish and Lynnette Wilfling.

Finally a very special acknowledgment is due to a colleague, Barbara Ludwig, for her research, interviewing of students, and most of all, her professional input.

Contents

Introduction

What is the "typical" American family? Judging by the television commercials and sitcoms, it is a family with two parents and a couple of children living together in a comfortable home. But government statistics paint quite a different picture. They show that the single-parent family is becoming more and more common. In fact, during the past three decades, the single-parent family has increased 450 percent. More than half of all teenagers live, or have lived, in a single-parent home. The trend toward single parenting is expected to continue throughout the rest of the century. By the year 2000 it is estimated that 70 percent of teenagers will be living in a single-parent household.

Despite the statistics, television images still maintain the myth of the two-parent nuclear family. According to myth, there has been no change in the way people approach marriage and family. In reality, marriage and family are radically changed. According to myth, parents always live with their children; in reality, one of the parents is likely to live apart from his or her children.

If you are trying to adjust to a single-parent home, the first thing you need to do is to review your own attitudes toward the myth and reality of family life. Perhaps your family was perfect until just a few weeks ago. Then again, perhaps it wasn't. In either case, you need to get used to the idea that you and your family are facing a time of change. Many teens have difeculty dealing with the situation because they hold onto the image of the two-parent nuclear family. You may feel that something went "wrong" in your situation, that you are somehow different or not "normal." You may become angry and confused, and fear the label "broken" or "dysfunctional." But there is nothing wrong with your family, and you are far from alone.

LONNIE'S STORY

Lonnie was thirteen and in the eighth grade. Her parents led busy lives. They both worked, and sometimes things got tense as everyone scrambled to get out of the house in the morning. Evenings could be difficult too. Her parents were tired and quick to anger. Lonnie assumed that they both were exhausted.

Now she realized the tension between her parents had another source. Just yesterday they had told her they were going to separate. Her father had found an apartment and would be moving there in the next few days. Legal proceedings had begun, and after a few months they would be divorced.

Lonnie's parents said they did not want to upset her life. She was going to live with her mother. Her father would see her every weekend. He was also going to call her every Wednesday to make sure they stayed in close touch.

But Lonnie felt her life *was* being upset. Everything she had thought okay, turned out to be not okay. The fights that had seemed minor were major. Her parents' "happy" marriage was an unhappy "mistake." She remembered days when she was little and they all went to the beach. Why couldn't it be like that anymore, she wondered. What was wrong with her family? Why couldn't they have a normal life?

Lonnie's feelings are understandable. It is hard to adjust to sudden change in your family structure. But the truth is that a single-parent home is neither abnormal nor "bad." About 60 percent are the result of divorce; 7 percent are caused by the death of one parent; and the other 33 percent are attributed to chronic illness, abandonment, and something new to the history of the family—deliberate choice.

CHOOSING PARENTHOOD

An increasing number of single men and women are *choosing* to become parents. Their behavior points to one of the reasons American family life has changed so dramatically. Single men and women have come to believe it is their right to raise children. Married men and women have come to believe it is their right to end a marriage, regardless of whether or not they have children.

All this gives individuals the freedom to search for personal fulfillment. It also creates uncertainty about the norms of family life. How will your life change? What exactly does living in a single-parent home mean? In some cases it can mean more responsibility and less free time. In other cases it may mean less money or a smaller house. You may have to move or switch schools. Or perhaps it means no outward change, just a growing awareness that your life with a single parent is different from those of your friends. Making the transition to a single-parent home, or coming to terms with it as a teen, can be difficult.

But have patience. Once you have adjusted to the idea, or settled into your new life, you will be able to enjoy it fully. The hardest part is making the first adjustments.

Reading this book will help. It is a guide to the issues you will face as an adolescent adjusting to divorce, abandonment, the illness or death of a parent, and single parenting without marriage. The more you know about the single-parent home, the better you will be able to cope with it.

CHAPTER 1

Single-Parent Homes

There are many young people like you living in a single-parent home. Statistics show us that many American households are changing their form, breaking away from the idea that a nuclear family must consist of two parents and children.

A few statistics make the trend toward single parent-hood very clear. About five years ago it was reported that 63 percent of seventeen-year-old black teenagers and 33 percent of seventeen-year-old white teenagers spent part of their childhood in a single-parent home. The figures for 1997 are expected to be higher: it is predicted that 80 percent of seventeen-year-old black teenagers, 56 percent of seventeen-year-old white teenagers, and 60 percent of seventeen-year-old Hispanic teenagers will spend part of their childhood in a one-parent home.

Each year more than 1 million babies are born to un-married women. That means that one third of all children come into the world with no father in the home. Many of these women choose to marry, but many more remain single.

From these statistics you can see that you are not unique as a young person who lives with only one parent. You are one of more than 16 million teenagers in single-parent families. These families live everywhere—in big cities and small towns, in rural areas and in suburbs, in rich neighborhoods and in poor. They are from all types of religious and ethnic backgrounds. Single-parent homes are filled with every type of person imaginable.

How do homes become single-parent households? The term "single-parent" has come to be associated mostly with divorce, with one parent still living but no longer at home. The 6 million such homes account for 60 percent of single-parent families in the United States.

A family headed by a single parent can also be the result of many other things, such as the death of one parent, a parent who never married, a single foster or adoptive parent, parental job requirements, or a parent having health problems. It is important to understand the circumstances of your living situation in order to meet the realities of day-to-day living.

Sixteen and one-half million children now live in single-parent homes in America. If they joined hands and formed a line, the line would stretch from Los Angeles, California, to London, England.

The main thing these children have in common is living with their mothers. Eighty-six percent of single parents are women. Many are divorced, but an increasing number have never been married. Today, 27 percent of all births are to unmarried women. This means that in 1996 more than 1 million babies were born to single mothers.

But the most surprising of all the changes in family life concerns men. Men are also becoming single parents in record numbers. During the last decade, the number of single fathers in the United States doubled. They now head 14 percent of single-parent homes. Most are divorced, but a significant number have chosen to be single parents. This trend is expected to continue and add to the growing number of single-parent households.

The new single-parent family faces many changes, some good, some bad. These changes come all at once and can be extremely stressful, because you as a teenager have little or no control over the situation. You may face a shortage of money, a new home, a change in schools, a change in your parent's personality, or perhaps more responsibilities. You may be asked to help solve your parent's personal problems. All this can be very disturbing.

Studies of single-parent families have shown that young people from one-parent homes seem to experience more problems than other teenagers. They have more difficulties in school. Because they are so upset by their changed situation, many of them earn low grades and are often late or absent.

So many changes in such a short time can be extremely difficult. However, you will come to the point in day-to-day living when you're strong enough to be responsible for your own actions and feelings. It's a tough task, but you will learn to deal with your new situation and move on with your life.

For some teens the inability to accept the changes in their lives leads to irresponsible behavior. Some teens can't handle the pain of their family situation, and instead of working through that pain they try to drown it in alcohol and drugs. But when the drugs are gone, the pain is still there. Getting into drugs and dropping out of school are merely escapes, not solutions for problems.

The task for you is to learn to take control of your emotions so you can begin feeling good about yourself. Now is the time to accept responsibility for your own life. You may want to seek help by talking things out with a friend, a school counselor, or a religious leader.

COMMUNICATING WITH YOUR PARENT

Some things about life in a single-parent home may seem hard; however, many other things can be unique and satisfying. Good communication between you and your parent will help you feel more at home, and in your life in general. Dialogue is the best way to keep good communications. Try to involve your parent in your life whenever possible; discuss both important and simple matters with your parent. Give his or her ideas and feelings the respect you want for your own.

The two of you won't see eye to eye on every issue; that's inevitable. But a dialogue will give you the opportunity to speak your mind. And once a dialogue is established, you may find that it is not very difficult to talk to your parent about personal feelings and to become closer. At the very least, you will be better informed about what's going on in the family.

FINANCES

Many families today have to watch their money carefully. And in single-parent families, this is often true as well. It can be difficult living in a situation like this, but there are many things you can do to help. Be patient with your parent and try to understand that there may not be enough money to go around. If you have the time, getting a part-time job can help you earn pocket money. Talk with your parent about other possible solutions. Telling your parent your concerns will let him or her know that you are thinking about the situation and ways to solve it.

IF YOU MOVE

Living in a single-parent home means that you may move in the near future. The neighborhood may be different, and you may have to transfer schools. New teachers, new classmates, a different principal—all these changes are hard to handle. It will help if you keep a positive outlook. New people mean new friends. A new neighborhood means new places to explore. Don't think you are going to lose your old friends; you can keep in touch with them through telephone, letters, and e-mail.

If you feel isolated, it is a good idea to take stock of your extracurricular activities. What are you interested in? Maybe it's music or sports. Risk taking the first step to try to meet other teenagers with the same interests. You might also think about developing a new interest, something you've always wanted to do but never have been able to try. Transitional periods in life are difficult, but they also provide opportunities for experimentation and growth.

YOUR IDENTITY

As a teen, the most important thing for you to do is to preserve your personal identity. When you are under stress, it is easy to get swallowed up by your problems. Try to remember that your first responsibility is to yourself. Separate *your* identity from the problems occurring between the adults in your family. Cultivating your extracurricular activities will allow you to express yourself and affirm your sense of individuality.

Your family is important, but so are you. You are growing and changing every day. Think about the person you want to be next year or two years from now. Make a plan for achieving the goal, whether it is getting into college or playing on the school football team.

YOUR PARENT'S BEHAVIOR

Being a single parent can be very demanding. Your parent probably has to juggle responsibilities at work and home that leave him or her frazzled by the end of day. Make an effort to understand and be patient. Your parent's moods are likely to be unpredictable: "Mom is up one day and down the next." And his or her general attitude towards things may change abruptly: "Dad always used to look at the bright side of things. Now, there's no pleasing him. He criticizes everyone and everything."

Take a good look at these changes in your parent. It is a good idea to try to see things from your parent's point of view. All these changes have pushed your parent into a many new situations, forcing him or her to take on extra responsibility. Talk to your parent and discuss how these changes are really upsetting or disappointing you.

Consider also that the rules may change now that your parent is alone. The rules that worked in the past—ideals, values, lifestyles—are being tested. This can lead to a great deal of frustration for both you and your parent. When you feel such frustration, try to consider it from your parent's point of view as well as your own.

Many teens find themselves being used by the single parent to "get back at" the other parent. A parent may act out all the anger that arises from being forced into the single-parent role, whether by divorce or separation. You as a teen can be caught up in a no-win situation. You get the punishment from two sides. Once again, don't be afraid to speak up. Get help from friends to work out what to say. Use all your favorite methods of persuasion, but tell both your parents not to drag you into their arguments. Explain how trapped you feel at being put in that situation. Ask them to solve their problems between themselves.

Some parents, however, exclude their children from all knowledge of family problems. They can be overprotective in trying to avoid involving you in family problems. Maybe your single parent doesn't believe you have the experience or background to understand complex matters. You are in the "in-between" years between childhood and adulthood, trying to assume some responsibility without taking the weight of the world on your shoulders. Tell your parent that you want to know what's going on. Often it's worse to hear about problems through rumors and neighbors than it is to hear them straight out.

If your problems are becoming too much to bear, try writing them down. Keeping a journal can help you organize your thoughts, and somehow writing down all your problems and fears seems to put everything in perspective. Later, you can look back at what you wrote and see how you solved your problems.

A CHANCE TO BOND

Living in a single-parent family isn't really all that bad. Many teenagers acquire new skills and become more self-reliant. Their relationship to the parent in the home often gains both strength and richness. They spend more time together, and come to find that they enjoy each other's company. In some cases, the bonding happens spontaneously; in others, the teenager and the parent have to make an effort. Realizing that you have the chance to bond is the important thing. Then you can take steps to develop a new kind of relationship with your parent.

Michael's Story

Michael's parents were divorced when he was twelve. Now, three years later, he lives with his mother during the school year and with his father during the summer. Though he and his mother don't argue much, they have drifted apart as he has become older and developed an interest in sports.

One night at dinner, she acknowledged her sense of distance. Michael agreed that they had become isolated from one another. He said she didn't like any of the things he enjoyed and didn't really try to understand his interests—perhaps, because she was always too busy. Would she, for example, ever sit down and watch a basketball game on TV?

He was surprised when she said that she would. Not the whole game, she added, but part of one if he explained the rules to her. And only if he reciprocated by watching part of a show she enjoyed. So they struck a deal. One week they would spend an hour together watching a sports event on TV. The next week they would spend an hour watching a show of her choosing, usually a drama or arts program.

After a few months, Michael realized that his relationship with his mother had changed in ways he really liked. He felt closer to her. When they talked now, it wasn't always about money and homework. They discussed the games and shows they had watched, and lately these conversations had led to other topics. Michael was proud of what they had accomplished. Their relationship had become more trusting and varied. His mother was still his mother, but she was also a special friend.

Building a Bond

Michael and his mother understood that they faced a choice. They could continue to drift further apart, or they could find a way to build a bond between them. The success of their effort surprised and pleased both of them. They felt they had taken a potentially negative situation and made it positive.

Living in a single-parent home has its ups and downs. So does a two-parent home. One is not necessarily better than the other. Recent studies suggest that the most important ingredient in family life is a sense of love and caring. When a child receives—and gives—that, the structure of the family matters very little. If there is one lesson to be learned from this book, it is to approach your life in a single-parent home with a positive attitude. It is the surest way to find the love and care you need and deserve.

CHAPTER 2

Divorce

F ifty-six percent of all children in America live, or will live, in a family that has gone through a divorce—that is 10 million people. Sixty percent of all single-parent families are created through divorce.

Take a minute and think about all the people you know who have been affected by divorce. How many of your friends live in single-parent homes? How many family members? The answer may surprise you.

If you're living in a single-parent home, however, the simple fact that you're not the only one probably doesn't make you feel any better about your situation. Divorce and separation result in many emotional and legal issues. Few teens are prepared for divorce when it happens. The shock, fear, feelings of uncertainty and insecurity, and grief over the loss of a parent can cause a lot of misery. Teenagers have talked about these feelings:

- Divorce or separation signals the collapse of the family structure; you feel insecure because the thing you most depended upon is gone.
- Parents going through divorce are involved in their own feelings. They frequently are unable to be the kind of parents you are used to.

- Divorce or separation creates conflicts of loyalty. You feel torn between your parents and feel guilt for not supporting them.
- When your parents divorce or separate, you begin to feel uncertain about many things. You become insecure about the future.
- Your parents probably are very angry and resentful. You may find yourself a little afraid of them. Feeling afraid makes you feel more alone.
- Dealing with the separation from one of your parents is a very difficult thing. If you are particularly close to that parent, divorce or separation can represent such a great loss that depression is often a natural reaction.

Going through a divorce, as a parent or a child, is highly emotional. Many issues need to be faced by everyone in the family. Talking about them, both beforehand and while they are happening, makes it easier to deal with even difficult problems. In divorce, however, that doesn't always happen; everyone may be too upset to talk or to listen. But ignoring problems doesn't make them go away. Chances are you will find yourself in situations you have little or no control over, don't like, and don't know how to change. Although you can't change the past, it might help you to understand what happened if you have a better grasp of what is going on around you.

WHAT IS A DIVORCE?

There are two kinds of divorce and separation: those that involve children, and those that don't. When there are no children, adults can divide up their material possessions and go their separate ways. When there are children, however, all kinds of other things have to be decided: with whom the children will live, where they will live, who will support them, and more.

Who decides all this? Many of the issues surrounding your life will be decided through the use of the legal system. A divorce or separation usually involves a lawyer, a legal document (a divorce decree) that represents the decision of both your parents, and sometimes a judge and a courtroom.

You probably have heard many confusing legal terms tossed around. After the divorce, fourteen-year-old Cheryl and her brother Sean lived with their mother except for weekends. They spent every Saturday and Sunday at their father's new apartment. It was fun having two places, and usually their father thought of really interesting things to do. But lots of times, when Cheryl and Sean got back to their mother's house, they felt confused and unhappy. Which place was home: the apartment or the house? Who decided where they lived? Why were they only permitted to stay with their father two days?

Their mother explained that the arrangement was part of the divorce settlement. It might not be ideal, but it gave everyone guidelines. Without the guidelines, life would be chaotic. No one would know where the children were supposed to be or when. And it would be hard for her and hard for their father to figure out how to allocate their time and financial resources. The divorce settlement, she said, took care of all those problems. It made certain that the children would see their father every weekend. It also set up guidelines about money and property that enabled them to get on with their lives.

The Divorce Decree

The rules for filing for divorce vary from state to state. In some states the parent filing must state why the divorce is necessary; these reasons given are the *grounds* for divorce. Some common grounds include the following:

- **No-fault divorce.** Neither party is at fault but the marriage is not working; a divorce is best for all members of the family.
- **Adultery.** One parent is having a sexual relationship outside of the marriage.
- **Cruel and abusive treatment.** One parent is abusing the other parent or their children, emotionally or physically or both.
- **Desertion.** One parent leaves the other by choice.
- **Nonsupport.** One parent refuses to support the other or the children or both.
- **Prison or jail sentence.** One parent is sentenced to prison, usually for more than five years.

Legal Orders

Legal orders are ways of dealing with emergencies that may come up before a divorce is final.

- **Temporary custody order.** One parent is given legal custody of a child until the divorce is final.
- **Temporary restraining order.** This prevents one parent from interfering with the other parent's safety or freedom. It might be needed to prevent one parent from harming the other or to force one parent to leave the home.
- **Temporary support order.** A judge can require that one of your parents (usually the one that has

left home) continues paying for things the family needs before the divorce is complete.

- **Temporary vacate order.** One of your parents is required to leave the home, usually because the parents are fighting or one parent is becoming physically or emotionally abusive to the other.

In some ways these orders sound more frightening than the divorce itself. It is important to remember that they are legal decisions and *must* be followed. But no lawyer or judge can tell families how they ought to feel. When parents are not getting along, emotions run high. Parents and kids may do or say off-the-wall things. These orders allow for a cooling-off time so that everyone in the family can back off and take a look at the situation more sensibly.

Mark, a fourteen-year-old, remembered hearing the words "temporary restraining order." His mom and dad were arguing about the new computer and "who got it." Mark said that after a long time of fighting his dad picked up a book and threw it at his mother. Mark went to his room, but when the police came he heard them talk about the restraining order his mother already had against his father. The police made his dad leave the house. From then on, Mark's dad couldn't even come on the front lawn. While confused at first, Mark said that at least if his parents fought they had to do it on the phone instead of in the house. He felt better about that.

Custody

Custody means that the court has assigned one of your parents guardianship (protection) of you while you are under the age of eighteen. There are several types of custody agreements:

- **Single-parent.** One parent takes full responsibility for the child, who lives with that parent all year.
- **Joint**
  1. Joint legal. Both parents share in making decisions about the child. Usually the child lives most of the time with just one parent.
  2. Joint physical. Both parents share the responsibility for decision making and for providing a home and caring for the child.
  3. Alternating. The child lives for periods of time first with one parent and then the other. An example is a child who lives with the mother during the school year and the father during the summer.
- **Third-party.** The court appoints a guardian, usually a relative or friend; this sometimes happens when neither parent wants or is able to take care of the child.

Cheryl and Sean's parents had joint legal custody. They had decided that it was best for the children to live with their mother. Their father would be able to visit them or take them to his home on weekends. Every divorce involves some kind of custody agreement. Knowing what kind of custody your parents were awarded in their divorce decree may help you understand why you live where you do, and when and how you see your noncustodial parent. For instance, Cheryl and Sean might not have been as upset with their mother if they had understood that their dad had agreed to be able to see them only on weekends.

Alimony

Alimony is payment made by one parent to the parent with whom you live the greater part of the year. The money allows your parent to live almost as well as before the separation or divorce. People married for a long time want more alimony than child-support money (described in the next section). Alimony amounts are decided at the time of divorce and are paid until the person paying dies or the person receiving the money remarries.

Child Support

Child support is payment made to the parent with whom you live. The money is to help pay for your food, clothing, and medical/educational expenses. Child support is considered as belonging to you and must be used for your needs. The court decides the amount, considering the income of the parent who pays.

If the parent fails to pay (which happens often), that parent can be called into court to explain why, and actually sent to jail for continued failure. Child support stops when you reach the age of eighteen.

Most single-parent families have less money after a divorce than before. The lack of money can cause hard feelings all around. It is important for you to realize that child-support payments are to be used to help your custodial parent with living expenses as well. You may look at the money as a new pair of tennis shoes; your mom may view it as helping pay for your telephone bill or braces.

YOUR ROLE IN DIVORCE

Your role in the legal issues surrounding a divorce may depend on how well you understand the family's problems, how much you feel you need to be involved, *and* how your parents feel about your input. Sometimes parents don't want their children involved. They may want to protect you from being hurt. Many of the things decided in the divorce decree will have quite an effect on your life. If you want to know what is going on, you are probably mature enough to talk to your parents about these legal things. Depending on your age (usually over fourteen), the court may even take your ideas into consideration, so as long as they are sensible. Your interest and concern may make a difference.

DENZIL'S STORY

"Last time my parents fought, it was about who I'd spend the weekend with. Know what? I don't think either one of them wanted me. Why didn't they just say so?" asked sixteen-year-old Denzil. Denzil was angry, but he was also hurt and insecure. Since he felt all those things and also felt rejected, he ran out of the house without telling his parents where he was going. He didn't come back until late that night. By then his parents were very concerned for his safety, and angry with him for being so inconsiderate; Denzil didn't feel much better either.

When asked how he dealt with facing two angry parents, Denzil said, "I went to bed!" Denzil belongs to a youth support group that deals with issues like this, along with many others. When asked by the group what he thought he could have done better, Denzil said that running away only aggravated the situation and made everyone more angry. Denzil *was* hurt, angry, and insecure, but he didn't tell anyone that, including his parents. He later said what he should have done was to tell his parents while they were arguing, "Wait a minute! You guys are making me feel like I'm not wanted—and that really makes me feel lousy!"

The best way to deal with your feelings is to talk about them. Communicate with your parents, your friends, a counselor, a group. Talk to someone who will listen. If nothing else, write them down in a journal or even on a loose sheet of paper. Once you have identified situations that make you feel angry or insecure, you can decide what to do about those situations. You can avoid them, confront and try to stop them, or learn to accept and deal with them. Avoiding a problem is usually not the best solution, but sometimes if you cannot change the situation, avoiding it gives you time to think about it. Do not just sit on your feelings or try to pretend the problems aren't there. They *are* there, and ignoring them doesn't make them go away; it just makes them fester. Do your best to work them out.

There are also bad ways of dealing with your feelings. Even though you know this, sometimes you can't help yourself and react rather than thinking things out. Don't take your anger out on other people or on your grades at school. Play basketball, sit down and draw, write a story, or play a game. Having problems with your parents or family is hard, but you can't let it ruin your life, your fun, and your relationships with them. That only makes things worse.

While you are getting better at dealing with your feelings, you might want to realize that your brothers and sisters, even your parents, are having the same trouble. Lending a helping hand, or ear, can make a big difference in your life as well as theirs. Think about offering to talk or listen the next time someone you care about is stressed. Sometimes giving help is as important as receiving it.

LIFE AFTER DIVORCE

Parents Change

The people you have become used to in your life will change, just as you will. It may take time to adjust and understand those changes and learn to deal with them.

Brian, a seventeen-year-old, remembered that his mother changed a lot. "She used to be always smiling and joking. She had a lot of friends over on the weekend for coffee and stuff. Now she never does anything and is always grumpy and yelling at me. No matter what I do she gets mad. She acts like it's my fault that Dad left!"

Barbara is sixteen years old. She and her twelve-year-old sister Lucy share a room and fight often. Before the divorce, their dad would make them sit down and try to work out agreements. Lately, he seems to have given up on them. Once, he walked out and did not come back until after midnight. Another time, he blew up: "I work all day and come home to this! I want peace and quiet. That's all I want, peace and quiet."

Life can be very explosive after a divorce. Parents and teenagers have bottled-up feelings. They are often under extreme strain as they try to adjust to new living arrangements. Don't be surprised if you or one of your parents or siblings loses control. Blowups are not always bad. Sometimes they are the only way people can admit something is bothering them. If you are involved in a blowup, don't be frightened and don't condemn the other people. In some situations, anger is justified and needs to be expressed. If any comments seem way out of line, wait a day or so until you and everyone else has had a chance to calm down. Then say you would like to discuss the blowup. You may need to apologize; then again, maybe your brother or sister or parent needs to apologize to you. But don't ignore the blowup. Sort out the issues causing the tension. Look at everyone's part in the situation. Try to understand one another's feelings and needs.

What if you are in a situation like Brian's where you think you're being forced to take the blame for the divorce? You may be misreading your parent's behavior. Teenagers often feel guilty after a divorce and think they caused it. It is important to remember the divorce is *not* your fault. A divorce is not between parents and children; it is between husband and wife. If you still think your parent is being unfair, confront him or her with your feelings. Sooner is better than later. The parent may not be aware of his or her behavior. It may actually be a disguised plea for help and affection. Whatever the sources of the parent's behavior, you are doing yourself and him or her a big favor when you say, "Let's talk about what's going on. You've changed."

Relatives Change

Before a separation or divorce, your family, relatives, family friends, and your "buddies" have been pretty much the same. This may also change. When your parents divorce, their families and friends may "get into the act." That can cause conflict and more problems for your mother and father and you. Family members have a natural urge to help, which means they may take sides. Family holidays, vacations, even such simple things as telephone calls can become strained, and it may suddenly seem that you have to make choices. Bobby, fifteen, said that one Thanksgiving he and his brother Sam had three places to go: to Dad's, with Mom and her friends, or with Dad's parents. They were told they could "choose" what they wanted to do. They felt really trapped; no matter what decision they made, somebody was bound to get hurt. In such situations it is important not to get caught in the middle. Bobby said they called their dad and grandparents, explained the situation, and said they didn't want to make that kind of decision because they wanted to go to all three. Bobby and Sam asked their mom to have the adults work it out and give them the decision.

It is especially important with close family members, grandparents, aunts, and uncles that you try to help them realize that the divorce has nothing to do with your actions. Sometimes relatives may associate you with the parent they feel is to blame. It's important for you to make them see that you are not either of your parents, and that you are not at fault for the divorce. If you make them realize that you still care about them and want them to care about you, it may clear the air a little. You should be able to love whomever you want without fear of anger, guilt, or rejection. However your relatives may feel about your parent, they have no right to impose their feelings on you.

Often relatives take sides, and speak critically about one of your parents in front of you. This is likely to anger you, and you may want to speak up to defend your parent. It can be good to make sure your relatives know how you feel; however, if they insist on putting your parent down, you should feel free to express your point of view. You do not need to be confrontational. In fact, quiet confidence is generally more effective than anger. Simply remind your relatives that they are talking about a parent you love and respect. You don't need to try to persuade them to see your parent the way you do. But you *are* entitled to ask that they stop criticizing your parent in your presence.

One of the hardest things to accept is that sometimes friends of the family feel an urge to take sides. Some of these friends may be closer to your mother, some to your father. When divorce occurs your parents naturally turn to their friends for support. When that happens, these friends may be torn between your parents and feel they have to choose between them. For example, a friend may decide to support your father, which may make your mom feel angry and hurt. Be aware that your parents want and need support from their friends. Expect changes in your parents' circle of friends—changes that could affect you, since you may see more, or less, of people who have become a familiar part of your life. Remember that these people are not deserting you but are responding to the needs of your parent. You may find it useful to treat these friends of the family in the same manner as your relatives. Explain to them that you are not an extension of either parent. Stress the fact that you are an individual and they should treat you as such. Simple things like being friendly when you see them, remembering birthdays with a card or phone call, and trying to keep in touch will help. However, you will often have to take the first step with relatives and friends, not wait for them to come to you. Extending yourself a little can be well worth the risk of being snubbed.

If Your Parent Starts to Date

While we're on the subject of people, it is highly likely that one or both of your parents will start to date.

Alicia's Story

Sixteen-year-old Alicia and her friends were up late one night watching TV when her mom came home with a man. Alicia hadn't even known that her mom had gone out on a date. It was pretty clear that both her mom and her date were surprised to find the girls still up. The man tried to be friendly, but Alicia was embarrassed and angry. She stormed off to her room and slammed the door. She didn't like the man and didn't like the idea of her mom dating or bringing him home to "her" house.

Having your parents date may not be much fun for you. While it's natural for them to move on to new relationships, your feelings about those relationships may vary. Just as your parents are a little hurt or jealous when you spend less time with them than with your friends, you may feel the same way. To feel a bit hurt or jealous is natural, but to nurse that hurt or jealousy until the negative feelings become a part of your life will lead to nothing but unhappiness. Talk to your mom or dad. Don't make excuses for your feelings; just explain them. If you don't talk things over, you may start to take it out on your parent by being rude to these new people who come to your home. That kind of behavior won't make them go away and won't make you feel any better. You can't "get even" with anyone through stupid or rude behavior.

Alicia's mother continued to see her new boyfriend. Alicia continued to be rude. One day she and her mom got into a big fight about it.

Mom: You don't seem to think I should have any men friends, Alicia. You don't want me to date or bring men home.

Alicia: If you mean that guy you've been seeing, you're right. He's weird. Anyway, it's my home too.

Mom: Okay. You want things to be equal. Think about this: You have your friends over to the house all the time. You go to movies with Ron, and he's over on the weekends to study or goof around. Do you want to make a deal? Neither of us will have men or boys in this house? Isn't that fair?"

Alicia didn't answer. That wasn't what she had in mind. Her mother went on, "You see, Alicia, you need your own friends, male and female. So do I. It certainly doesn't mean that I love you any less, or you me, because we want to do things with our friends, does it?"

You probably see the point. Your parents need their own friends, and they need to spend time with them. At first it may seem that they spend too much time away from you. They need to learn to balance time with friends and with family, just as you do. You don't have to like your parents' friends, but it will make life a lot easier if you understand that they need them. This may sound like a broken record, but keeping your feelings a secret is not the answer to this problem. Talking helps.

Places Change

Will the "places" in your life change? Could be; it depends mostly on the custody decision. You may have two homes from now on (one with Mom, one with Dad), and that could take some getting used to. If your parents' divorce means that you move to another part of town or another city, give your new neighborhood a chance. Take time to get used to the changes. After all, you might even find that you prefer your new situation to your old one. If you are determined not to like it, you won't, and you will make yourself miserable. The odds are that you can't change this decision, so the best thing to do is accept it and make the best of it.

To understand why the places in your life have changed, you need to know some things about your parents' divorce. Often the court has decided where and with whom you will live. The divorce decree may also specify whom you can visit and for how long. In the Andersons' divorce the kids stayed with their mom during the school year but went to another city to spend the summer with their dad. Fifteen-year-old Jill's parents switched weekends; she was with her mom two weekends in a row (he also lived with her), and then with her dad for the next two weekends. Knowing this in advance can help you plan ahead. It's also a good idea to be sure your parents know your plans so they can consider them.

Seventeen-year-old Kate's dad came to pick her up one Friday afternoon, and she didn't want to go. She had been asked to the school prom but hadn't told him about it. Her dad had arranged some fun things for them to do together over the weekend and was mad when he found out about the dance. He felt that Kate or her mother should have called him. Was he right to have been angry? What could have prevented this? Everyone is busy and has plans. It is common courtesy to tell your parents about your plans; it gives them time to change their schedules, if possible. After that weekend Kate made an agreement with her dad to send him her school schedule and ideas about activities and dates. That worked well; it made Kate's life easier, and her dad felt less left out.

There may be times when you don't want to spend a weekend or summer with one of your parents. You want to change the plans. You need to realize that many things in your schedule were decided in the divorce decree. Begging to get your way or throwing a tantrum is not the answer. It only makes things difficult for both your parents and puts a strain on your relationship with them.

You also need to know that the court usually requires that your noncustodial parent get permission from your custodial parent in order to take you out of the state or to a foreign country. Trips of more than thirty days may mean that only one parent gets to see you. The court may not allow that unless both of your parents agree.

Having a court decide what you can and cannot do can be frustrating. If things are really impossible, you might ask your parents to consider your ideas about changes in the custody or visitation and vacation rights. Such changes need to be negotiated. Be reasonable. As mentioned before, courts are usually willing to listen to children over fourteen if their ideas make sense. However, going to court should be a last resort. First try to balance things with your parents.

Situations Change

Did you know that in eleven out of twelve divorces the courts award custody of children to the mother? Statistics indicate that these new families are often at a financial disadvantage. The court usually awards them less than half the husband's income, and most husbands fall behind in their support payments. Even if your mother works, and 80 percent do, finances probably are going to be tight. Recent changes in government support for families with dependent children will make matters worse for numerous single-parent homes.

No one likes being short of money, least of all a parent trying to keep his or her family together. If your parent seems worried or irritable, he or she may be worried about getting the car fixed or mounting credit card debt. You might be asked to hold down your expenses. Your parent might even say you have to spend less on clothes and school supplies. If you have never earned any money before, now is a good time to try to pick up some work. The amount you earn is likely to be small, but it will help cover some of your personal expenses. Make a list of jobs you could do and try to find a way to do one of them.

Crystal, aged fourteen, and a friend set up a baby-sitting service. They called it "Really Great Kids." One Saturday they worked together to design a flyer listing their names, telephone numbers, and hourly rate. After they copied it on a copier, they distributed it to neighbors and posted it on the bulletin boards at nearby churches. They soon were busy every weekend, making at least $25 each. The money was useful, and they were proud of their business. It gave them a feeling of independence.

There are other ways to ease the financial pressure on you and your family. Take good care of possessions. They will last longer, and your parent will spend less on repairs and replacements. Help more around the house; for example, you could offer to go through the grocery ads, clipping coupons and making a list of sale items. Cooking can be fun and a way to save money, and almost anything made at home is cheaper (and better) than take-out or pre-prepared. Besides, once you are on your own, you'll be glad you learned how to prepare an inexpensive dinner. Ask your parent for other suggestions. If he or she is reluctant to discuss the financial crunch with you, explain that you want to help. Add that not knowing and not helping make you more, not less, anxious about the situation.

Some teenagers face quite a different problem. They have what are called "Santa Claus parents."

The parents' motto is "Spend money, buy love." They load their kids up with things, trying to buy their love and affection. Don't let yourself get caught in this trap. This sort of parent behavior will fill your room with goodies, but will it bring you love and affection? Buying you things cannot make up for the time the parent doesn't spend with you or the visits that are not made. If this is your situation, you have to make up your mind whether you want a lot of things or your parent's time and attention. It's not that the "Santa Claus parent" doesn't love you; he or she just doesn't realize that you would trade all the things in a second for a bit of attention. Speak up! Tell your parent how you feel. Explain that goodies can't take a parent's place.

Try not to get caught in the middle of a battle between your parents over who can give you the most. That kind of battle can bring nothing but hard feelings to everyone. Above all, learn to accept both of your parents for who, and what, they are. Whether they give you things, time, money, or love, accept them and value them equally.

Living in a single-parent family, you may find that you have too much or too little of what you want. Either way, as you become older and more independent you'll want to take more responsibility for yourself and work toward the things you want. The earlier you begin doing that, the better you will feel about yourself. It's a great feeling to know that you don't have to rely on everyone else for the things you want. You will have a real opportunity to "take charge" and contribute (through helping out or earning money) to your self-image, and your family.

Living in a single-parent family that is the result of divorce or separation can be rough at first. It's up to you to keep speaking out so that you can make your life go well for you. If you speak out, the people around you will begin to understand what you need from them. The more you try to work out your problems, and the more you communicate with your parent, the happier you will be. Remember, you cannot change the past, but you can control your own future. You can make your new home life miserable, or you can make it satisfying. Keeping cool, talking things out, and doing things for yourself instead of relying on or blaming others will take you a lot further than being bitter or angry. Millions of kids in America share your feelings. They've lived through a divorce; you will too. Take some action, take some time. Things *will* change for the better.

CHAPTER 3

Single Parenting
Without Marriage

t is often difficult for young people to understand how a mother or father might want to be a parent but not want to be a wife or husband. A lot of personal choice is involved in that kind of decision. Some adults think that choosing single parenting is not the best thing. After all, raising a child is tough; why would anyone want to do it alone? Other people think it's the best thing to do, because they then can devote their full attention and love to their children without being distracted. If you're living in a single-parent home where that decision was made, you probably have your own feelings about it. But the important thing is to take charge of your life, not to spend time worrying about how you came to be a member of a single-parent family.

Growing up in a single-parent family, you will be spared the shock and stress that come from divorce. You do not have to readjust to a new type of home; your home was always run by one parent. Nevertheless, sometimes it can be difficult to cope with this family structure.

It may help to remember that you're not the only teenager living in a single-parent home. The most recent statistics show that nearly 3 million children under the age of eighteen live in a single-parent home with a parent who was never married. More than 2 million of these families are headed by single mothers, and single fathers head about 343,000 of them.

FAMILY CHOICES

What makes some single-parent households different from others is that these parents choose to remain single and to have or adopt a child. Family choices have changed greatly over the years. Single motherhood is no longer the taboo it was just thirty years ago. As a result, many more mothers are deciding to have children without having a husband. Some of these mothers bear a child; others adopt one. Men's attitudes toward parenting also have changed in recent years. It used to be rare for a single man to take on responsibility for a family. Now, more and more men are adopting children or seeking, and receiving, custody of children they have fathered outside marriage. The number of single-father homes has doubled during the last decade.

People decide to be single parents for different reasons. Some want to experience the joy and happy times of having a child in their life and feel they have a lot of love to give. Others believe that they can do more for a child than a foster home or an institution can, so they open their heart and home to a child.

Regardless of the reason for the decision, all of these parents had one thing in common: They were ready to accept the single-parent situation. That doesn't mean that it never had its ups and downs, but at least they were ready to cope without a spouse. Maybe they had friends to give support when they couldn't handle problems alone; or maybe they had a close family around to pitch in to help. They were able to find ways to hang in there during times when they may have doubted their choice.

Where does that leave you? You didn't choose to have only one parent; you grew up that way. You might find that with adolescence, problems crop up in the family that you have never had before. You might begin to wonder unnecessarily if you are abnormal because you have only one parent. You may become insecure about your status. You may be wondering what happened to your other parent, and where he or she is now. If you are adopted, you might wonder who and where your birth parents are.

Part of growing up and part of being a teenager is finding out *who* you are: What are your values? How do you feel about issues in the world? What kind of adult do you want to be? The specific circumstances of why you were born or how your family was formed are not as important as the kind of love and support you received while growing up. In other words, who you are is affected by the things that have happened since you became a part of your family; knowing all the details of what happened to make you a part of your family doesn't change who and what you are.

IF YOU LIVE WITH YOUR MOTHER

During the last decade, the number of single, never-married mothers has tripled. There are many reasons why so many women are becoming single parents. Often, a woman chooses to have a child on her own. There are any number of reasons why she may not want to marry the father of her baby. Maybe the two of them were too young to be serious about marriage; maybe he wasn't someone she cared for enough to live with forever; maybe she didn't think he would be a good father. She may have realized that it takes much more than having a child together to make a marriage. So she chose to be a mother and not a wife.

Some women plan to have a baby when they reach a certain age. If they haven't found the person they want to marry by that time, they still carry out plans for a child. They are usually in their thirties by the time they start a family and often have a career and a substantial income. Motherhood appeals to them as a way to share their life with someone.

A teenager who lives with his or her mother may know the father but not keep in touch with him or may have no knowledge of him. Suppose you're a teenager who lives with your single mother and wants to know about your father. Where could he be? Do I look like him? Does he like the things that I do?

Many psychologists say these questions should be explored, although the process might prove difficult. It can bring up memories that might be sad or painful for both you and your parent. You may have to deal with past disappointments; you may be surprised by the stories you hear or don't hear. Some single mothers—and single fathers—don't want to talk about the other parent. You don't have to take no for an answer, but you should use a little tact. Wait for a few days before you raise the topic again. Be prepared for mixed feelings, some sad, some happy, when you do get the information you want. Your mother might make negative remarks about your father. Keep in mind that no one is all bad, just as no one is perfect.

Karen's Story

Karen has lived with her mother ever since she can remember. Until recently, she never thought much about her father. She sensed he was best left in the deep past. But now she is fifteen, has a boyfriend, and is curious about her father's personality and appearance.

When she first tried to talk to her mother about her father, her mother became tense. She said, "You're better off not knowing, believe me. Keep the past in the past." After a few days, Karen brought up the question again. This time, her mother agreed to talk. She said she realized that Karen needed to know and was old enough to deal with the truth.

She had met Karen's father when she was eighteen and had fallen in love with him right away. He was older, handsome, and knew how to make her laugh. When they started to live together, she discovered he was a dreamer who had trouble accepting responsibility. He also experimented with drugs. They talked about marriage, but Karen's mother decided that, in the long run, it wouldn't work. A month before Karen's birth, they broke up and agreed not to see each other again.

Truth Brings Relief

Karen and her mother were quiet for a while. Finally, Karen said that knowing the truth was a relief. Her mother admitted that she too felt a burden had been lifted from her shoulders. Then she smiled and said, "It wasn't easy, but I'd do it all over again. We had such a great kid."

Karen will never know exactly what her father was like when her mother met him. Maybe her mother overemphasized his weaknesses. What Karen has learned is that he had a few problems. This is true of everyone; even so, learning that a parent is less than perfect can be upsetting. Karen's mother was wise to say she was glad she had her as a daughter. You can also see why some psychologists believe teens should question their single parents about the past. Karen experienced some sadness, but she gained insight into her situation and felt closer to her mother than ever before. She saw her mother as someone who kept a child but rejected a marriage.

IF YOU LIVE WITH YOUR FATHER

Karen's story might not be so very different if she lived with her father. Like a single mother, a single father faces some tough issues concerning marriage and family. Studies show that men make the choice to be single fathers for many of the same reasons single mothers do. They want to share their lives with a child. However, there is one big difference between single mothers and single fathers. Single fathers are breaking a gender stereotype. They take on child-care duties long reserved for women. Their behavior is part of the sweeping changes in attitudes toward the family. Men in two-parent families are also taking a larger part in bringing up children. The majority report that the change is gratifying. They enjoy the interaction and feel closer to their children. Single fathers say their experience is similar. They enjoy taking care of the family and feel more fulfilled.

Some teenagers who live with their fathers maintain regular contact with their birth mothers. But because the mother is unavailable or unwilling, many others do not.

Often, they have questions about her; questions like those Karen had about her father. They want to know about their mother's personality, her appearance, and her hobbies. Why isn't she around more? If you feel this way, you might ask your father if he has any photographs of your mother. It is a good way to start a conversation about earlier days. He may not have photographs of your mother, and he may not want to discuss her. You won't know until you ask. He may be waiting for you to raise the issue, not because he is shy or angry, but because he wants you to be ready to deal with the information. If you ask, it is a sign that you'll be able to understand the decisions he and your mother made.

David's Story

David, thirteen, was happy living with his father. He was also close to his grandparents who lived nearby. But there were moments when he wondered why his mother never called or came to visit. He felt rejected by her, though he would never dare to say so. Finally, one evening, when he felt a little down, it just came out. He asked his father what had happened to his mother. Did he have a photo of her?

After a few minutes, his father said, "No, no photo, but there is lots to tell and now is as good a time as any." Her name was Helen and she was a "free spirit." Even before she became pregnant, she was having trouble settling down in her relationship with David's father. She wanted to travel, to find a new kind of lifestyle, and to let go of the past. David's father said he saw things differently. He liked staying in one place and wanted to have a home and family. So they agreed that Helen would have the baby and that he would take full responsibility for the baby's care.

"It was a painful decision," David's father said, "but it had nothing to do with rejection." The issues were all about choice. David's mother chose one way of life; his father chose another. David's father added that it was the smartest thing he had ever done. He wouldn't trade a minute of his experiences with David for anything in the world.

David realized that both his parents were "free spirits." They had strong ideals and tried to live them out. It takes courage to be honest about your ideals when they don't fit into norms of behavior. Helen wanted to explore the world on her own—something that used to be denied to women; David's father wanted to raise a child on his own—something that used to be often denied to men. When people strike out in new directions, their friends and relatives get confused. They might feel rejected the way David did until he talked with his father. There is nothing wrong with confusion. What's wrong is not taking steps to clarify your thoughts and feelings.

Whether you are living with your father or your mother, ask questions about his or her attitudes toward family and marriage. Think of your parent as a pioneer on the frontier of society. You are on that frontier too, and the more you know about it the happier you will be.

WHAT IF YOU WERE ADOPTED?

Another type of never-married, single-parent family comes about through adoption. Statistics show that many more single adults are adopting children than ever before. Men and women are realizing that they can provide a loving home for a child who otherwise might not have one. The children are generally American, but adoption in America can be a slow process. Several foreign countries have less red tape and more children in need of homes. During the last decade, many more of these children have been adopted and brought to America by men and women eager to have families.

Confidential Adoption

Some parents choose to tell their children they are adopted; others choose not to. If you have been told you were adopted, you should ask if the adoption was open or closed. A closed adoption is the same as a confidential one.

Almost all adoptions in America used to be confidential. When an adoption is confidential, the birth parents give the child to an agency. The agency then selects the child's new family. The agency does not tell either set of parents anything about the other. The record of the adoption is sealed permanently: no one is allowed to go to the agency and look up information about the adoption.

Confidentiality is not as strange as it appears. The rules have a purpose. Remember that bearing a child outside marriage used to be taboo. Until recently, most adopted babies came from unmarried mothers who wanted to remain anonymous.

Open Adoption

Open adoptions are fast becoming the preferred form of adoption. When an adoption is open, the birth parents and adoptive parents disclose their identities to one another— to the extent to which both parties feel comfortable. No two open adoption agreements are the same. Sometimes the adoptive parents and birth parents decide to set up a "blended family." Everyone exchanges regular visits and the child grows up knowing his or her birth parents and adoptive parents. Sometimes the birth parents and adoptive parents keep their lives separate. There are no visits; the adoptive parents might send photos and progress notes to the birth parents. The agreement may cover the first few months of the child's life; it may cover the child until he or she reaches eighteen. It may also change several times as the child grows up.

Open adoption is new, and the arrangements are flexible. Birth fathers do participate, but usually the birth mother plays the leading role. Take a moment to think about the change in attitudes this represents. Once, when an unmarried mother placed her child for adoption, she had to surrender all her rights to the child. Now, she can choose to stay in contact with the child and have her identity fully recognized.

Understanding Your Adoption

If your adoption was open, there is a good chance you know one or both of your birth parents; then again, you might not. The agreement may have covered only your first year or excluded visits. If your adoption was confidential, you will have little or no knowledge of your birth parents. This is usually the case also for an international adoption. Teenagers tend to be curious about birth parents they have never met. Often, they idealize them. They imagine them as movie stars, or rich and famous. They try to figure out ways to find them and have a happy reunion. Other adolescents want to find their birth parents because they feel they don't really "belong" in their adoptive families. They feel "different" and think their birth parents will make them feel normal.

If you are confused about your identity, meeting one or both of your birth parents may help you, but the help may include some surprises. Teenagers react in many different ways when they come face to face with a birth parent they have never met. Some form a loving relationship with the birth parent and blend him or her into their adoptive families. For other teenagers, the birth parent becomes a good friend; others prefer to meet their birth parent only once. Nearly all continue to regard their adoptive parent as their "real" mother or father.

B.J.'s Story

B.J.'s real name was Bruce James. His friends and his mother—his adoptive mother—called him B.J. He found out he was adopted five years ago when he was eleven. He has felt a little "different" ever since and wondered about his birth parents. He knew his birth mother was seventeen when she had him and now lived in another part of the country. One evening the telephone rang. After a couple of minutes, his adoptive mother took the cordless telephone into her study and closed the door.

Later that evening, she told B.J. his birth mother had called. She was going to call again and hoped to talk to him. B.J.'s mother said he had a decision to make and only he could make it. When the phone rang again he picked it up. His conversation with his birth mother went well. A few weeks later, she came to visit. She showed him photographs of her other children and told him about her life. She said she was sorry she had lost contact with him after the adoption.

B.J. was nervous at first. He didn't know what to call her. They decided he'd call her by her first name, Judy. After Judy left, B.J. decided he didn't want to set up a blended family with her and her other children. He wrote her a letter saying he'd prefer to send her a progress note twice a year and not exchange visits.

B.J. liked Judy and was glad they had finally met one another. But he realized that he had bonded with his adoptive mother. She had taken care of him for sixteen years and had become his "real" mother.

If you were in B.J.'s position, what would you do? Perhaps you would decide to try to bond with your birth mother. Keep in mind that some adoptive parents feel threatened when a birth parent appears on the scene. They fear they are going to lose you to your birth parent. If this is the case, you might find yourself juggling the love and the demands of both your adoptive parent and your birth parent.

What if you are adopted and don't know your birth parents? You should think about B.J.'s story. It won't stop you from wondering about your birth parents, but it will help you put things in perspective. You do have a "real" parent. This is also true if you and your adoptive parent have different racial and ethnic backgrounds. Over the years you've been together, you've become parent and child. The bond doesn't need to exclude awareness of racial and ethnic differences. Ask your parent about it. When people acknowledge differences, they feel happier about their relationships. They feel they are helping strengthen each other and becoming more self-aware.

YOUR GENDER IDENTITY

Teenagers who live with one parent tend to wonder how life would be with the other parent. These thoughts come more often when a son lives with his mother or a daughter lives with her father. Each thinks a parent of the same gender might be more understanding about things like sex and dating. Teenagers also get concerned about their parent's understanding of male or female identity. They worry that they won't know how men behave if they live with their mother. If they live with their father, they worry that they won't know how women behave. When their parent is gay or lesbian, they have questions about the development of their own sexual preferences.

Don't hesitate to ask your parent about these issues. As single persons who chose to be parents, they have probably thought them through. You might discover they can answer all your questions. The two of you might decide that you should get a mentor of the opposite gender. A relative or one of their friends might be willing to spend time with you. Many teens in single-parent homes develop a network of older friends and relatives who provide companionship and advice. If you don't have access to a network and you feel the need to talk to an adult other than your parent, try a coach or a teacher. If that doesn't work, call one of the organizations listed at the end of the book. The organizations are there to help teenagers like yourself. But to get the help, you need to take the first step. Call or write. Chances are you'll be glad you did.

All of us love to tell our own life stories from beginning to end. But what might seem to be a missing part—a parent you don't know—may not really be missing at all. Perhaps your story is just different from some of the others. You don't have a chapter on Dad, but you have lots more information on Mom. You didn't grow up with a mother or father, but you grew up with a parent who cared enough to make you a part of the family. As time goes on, you'll realize that what's important is not what you *don't* have in your life, but what you *do* have.

CHAPTER 4

When a Parent Leaves Without Saying Good-Bye

L earning to deal with the absence of a parent is a difficult task. But when one of your parents leaves without warning or even a good-bye, your whole family may be thrown into a state of confusion. Many different feelings overwhelm the spouse and children who are left behind. Finding ways to handle these emotions can make it easier to accept what has happened.

When parents divorce there is usually time to prepare yourself for the day when one of them leaves. You have time to think over how you are going to keep in touch with that parent. But when the end of your parents' marriage is marked by one parent's desertion, you have no chance to prepare—one day the parent is here, the next day, gone. It is scary not knowing where your mom or dad is or whether he or she is ever coming back. Maybe it will help to know something about parents who leave the family. If you know why, the "What am I going to do?" question may be easier to answer.

UNDERSTANDING DESERTION

Government officials have difficulty estimating the number of parents who leave home. Many such parents will do almost anything to keep from being found. If they call to reassure their families, it may be from a number that can't be traced. Being found may mean being forced to face the problems they ran from in the first place, so they become experts at hiding. Try not to spend too much time daydreaming about how you're going to find your parent. It can be disappointing, as well as a waste of your time and energy.

Many people say that a parent who runs away is morally wrong. After all, everyone has problems, but not everyone quits. If someone does quit by running, he or she must be a weak or a bad person. Don't believe that! Some parents cannot handle all the problems of a family; that doesn't make them weak or bad. Try to come up with a fair answer as to why your parent left, one that you can live with without hating your parent.

Rather than *choosing* to run, some people actually *need* to run. They need time away to help them calm down and sort out the confusion in their lives. When they get a grip on things they may come back. Of course, some never quite get a grip or finish sorting things out, so they keep running.

YOUR FEELINGS

Kara's father left when she was twelve years old. He called the family from pay phones to "check on them" and promised to come by to see them once he got his act together. But two and a half years later he is still trying to "work things out." Kara has gone from hoping her father will return to feeling angry. She has gone on with her life and wishes now that he would stop playing games and just admit he's not coming home.

In some families, divorce is not acceptable because of religious beliefs or the feeling that it is a cowardly way out of a mess. To leave is an easy way out of the family troubles and the social, emotional, or financial costs of a legal divorce. But the parent who leaves ignores the fact that the family members left behind pay a terrible price for a long time. Running away is selfish when you look at it this way. The one who leaves takes the easy way out and you're left with the tough part—a part you didn't choose.

Some people blame the parent left behind for not having made the spouse happy. Some children even blame themselves or each other for being "bad" and making the parent want to leave. That is simply not true. The troubles and problems are caused by the parents who run away. If they can't find the strength to deal with whatever makes them unhappy and restless, they take off. No one made them go, and no one can solve their problems but themselves.

Jake is a fifteen-year-old whose father left four years ago. On holidays throughout the year he would come home and stay for a few days. Jake and his younger brother and sister used to think that each visit might be that special time Dad would stay for good, but it never happened. Every time he would leave again, the kids would blame each other. But that wasn't right. Jake realizes now that it wasn't their fault; nothing could have made their dad stay.

FINANCES

Money is always a touchy problem when a parent deserts the family. Parents who leave sometimes withdraw money from bank accounts, either slowly or all at once. To disappear is an easy way to avoid paying family expenses.

If your family was left with little or no money, you may need to think a little differently about how much you spend. Let's say that your mom left and took half of the family savings with her. Your dad may not want to tell you this because he thinks you will worry. If you believe that is the case, you should talk to your dad and let him know that you are willing to help out in some way. If you talk to him in a mature way, he'll probably be relieved that he doesn't have to hide the truth from you any longer. Then perhaps you can decide how best to handle the shortage of money.

Ana was seventeen when her mother left and withdrew all the money from the family's checking account. When Ana found out that her dad was worried about money, she offered to take a lunch to school instead of buying one, and she baby-sat more often on weekends instead of going out. She also started helping with the grocery shopping by cutting coupons and watching the newspaper for sales. Ana's dad appreciated her help and felt good about having a daughter who could handle things so well. Every little bit helps when your parent has to take on money worries that were not exactly planned.

ADJUSTING TO YOUR SITUATION

What can you do to turn the situation of being left behind into one that you can live with? In addition to money issues, there are many emotional issues to face. You may be worried about the parent who left, wondering if something has happened. It's hard to accept that a parent would stay away voluntarily. Some teenagers in such a situation check the newspaper every day for reports of car accidents. They even call hospitals in case their parent has been hurt and has no identification. Eventually this kind of search is given up; anxiety and fear give way to other feelings as time goes on.

You may feel angry at your parent for leaving without even saying good-bye. Some parents who leave tell a friend or two that they are thinking about it, but others don't tell anyone. You should never feel that if you had known you could have stopped it. Remember, your parent left because of personal feelings. You cannot control what is inside another person no matter how much you care.

Denise's Story

A day after her fourteenth birthday, Denise got a birthday card from her father. It didn't have a return address, but it did include a $20 bill. She tore up the card and the money and threw them away. Her father had disappeared six months prior without any warning. Denise felt hurt and angry, and the birthday card only made things worse.

That week she had a conference with her English teacher. He asked her what was happening in her life. Her grades had slipped, and she had stopped speaking in class. When she told him what had happened, he said she had two options. She could keep her emotions inside her and probably become more angry. Or she could try to find ways to express her feelings. He suggested that Denise try keeping a journal. That would give her the chance to say what was going through her head. He said that not being able to say anything to her father was probably one of the reasons she was so angry. She might not ever be able to tell her father how she felt, but she could write it out in her journal.

Though Denise didn't know if she believed her teacher, she decided to try keeping a journal. The first entry described her reaction to the birthday card from her father. After a couple of weeks, she realized the journal was helping her. She could say whatever she wanted, even if it wasn't nice. A few weeks after that, she noticed that her rage had eased up. There was something about writing how she felt that made her feel better about herself.

Find Someone to Trust

When a parent abandons his or her home, teenagers often suffer a loss of self-esteem. Feeling embarrassed about having one of your parents take off is also a normal reaction. How do you explain it to your friends? You may start by saying that your father took a job out of town or that your mother is visiting a sick relative. Such stories may buy you a little time, but your close friends will catch on after a while. If you don't want to keep a journal, find someone you trust and explain what has happened.

It's okay to let others help you get through this; you don't have to deal with it alone. Friends your age may make you feel better, but adults that you feel comfortable with, such as a school counselor or a coach, might be able to give you a different point of view to help you over some of the rough days.

You cannot deny the fact that your family has been upset and suddenly forced into a difficult situation. You may see changes in the parent who is still at home, changes you don't understand. Sometimes that parent becomes depressed and feels worthless, hurt, and rejected.

Be patient. Your parent's feelings may change over time. As those feelings start to turn to anger, the parent may snap at you or be very short-tempered. Try not to be too upset or angry about it. Talk to your parent about how *you* feel. If your family is to get through this, you need to talk and work together. Throwing blame around only hurts the rest of the family and causes bad feelings. Chapter 7 contains other helpful suggestions that might work in your specific situation.

When one of your parents leaves, you'll have to deal with many different things. It's best if you tackle just one at a time. Write down all the things you'll have to do differently and arrange them in order of importance. If your father drove you to baseball practice on weekends, but now he's gone, that should go on your list. Take one thing at a time and see what ways you can come up with to solve it. Again, it's okay to ask for help. Friends and family who care about you will do what they can to make all these big changes in your life easier.

It is natural for you to keep thinking that tomorrow your parent will come back for good, but you can't keep on kidding yourself. You have to admit that some parents leave home forever. You really must get on with your life, accepting the fact that this is how things will be from now on. Yes, it's painful to accept, but necessary if you want to be anywhere near happy again. It won't be easy to go on, but you can find the strength not to quit.

Often in situations like this the family keeps looking for the parent who has left, but that is usually a waste of time. It's better by far just to let go—but for those who cannot do that right away, some services that help families in the search are listed at the end of this chapter. For those able to accept their one-parent home life, keep trying to find ways that will make things better for all the family and especially for yourself.

The teen years are tough enough when everything is going smoothly. No one is saying that you can handle everything without ever needing help. But the things that you can do to take charge of some part of your life are there; you just need to find them with a little help. Talk to the parent who is still at home; go to other adults you trust for advice; don't keep away from your friends. Don't give up on yourself, because *you* can make a difference in your family's life as well as your own.

STATE CHILD SUPPORT ENFORCEMENT AGENCIES

ALABAMA
Bureau of Child Support
Alabama Department
  of Pensions and
  Security
50 Ripley Street
Montgomery, AL 36130
(205) 242-9300

ALASKA
Child Support Enforcement
  Division
Department of Revenue
550 West 7th Avenue
Anchorage, AK 99501
(907) 276-3441

ARIZONA
Child Support Enforcement
  Administration
Department of Economic
  Security
P.O. Box 40458—Site Code
  966-C
Phoenix, AZ 85067
(602) 253-5206

ARKANSAS
Division of Child Support
  Enforcement
Arkansas Social Services
P.O. Box 3358

Little Rock, AR 72203
(501) 371-2464

CALIFORNIA
Child Support Program
  Management Branch
Department of Social
  Services
744 P Street, Mail Stop
  9-011
Sacramento, CA 95814
(916) 322-8495

COLORADO
Division of Child Support
  Enforcement
Department of Social
  Services
717 17th Street
P.O. Box 181000
Denver, CO 80218-0899
(303) 294-5994

CONNECTICUT
Bureau of Child Support
  Enforcement
Department of Human
  Resources
1049 Asylum Avenue
Hartford, CT 06105
(203) 566-3053

DELAWARE
Division of Child Support
  Enforcement

Department of Health and
  Social Services
P.O. Box 904
New Castle, DE 19720
(302) 421-8300

**DISTRICT OF
COLUMBIA**
Office of Paternity and Child
  Support
Department of Human
  Services
425 I Street NW
Washington, DC
  20009
(202) 724-5610

FLORIDA
Office of Child Support
  Enforcement
Department of Health and
  Rehab Services
1317 Winewood Boulevard—
  Bldg 3
Tallahassee, FL 32399-0700
(904) 488-9900

GEORGIA
Office of Child Support
  Recovery
State Department of Human
  Resources
P.O. Box 80000
Atlanta, GA 30357
(404) 894-4119

GUAM
Child Support Enforcement
  Office
Dept. of Public Health andd
  Social Services
194 Hernan Cortez Avenue
Agana, GU 96910
(671) 477-2036

HAWAII
Child Support Enforcement
  Agency
Department of Attorney
  General
770 Kapiolani Boulevard
Honolulu, HI 96813
(808) 548-5779

IDAHO
Bureau of Child Support
  Enforcement
Department of Health and
  Welfare
Statehouse Mail
Boise, ID 83720
(208) 334-5710

ILLINOIS
Bureau of Child Support
  Enforcement
Illinois Department of Public
  Aid
P.O. Box 2127
100 South Grand Avenue East
Springfield, IL 62705
(217) 782-1366

INDIANA
Child Support Enforcement
  Division
Department of Public
  Welfare
141 South Meridian
  Street
Indianapolis, IN 46225
(317) 232-4885

IOWA
Bureau of Collections
Iowa Department of Human
  Services
Hoover Building
Des Moines, IA 50319
(515) 281-5580

KANSAS
Child Support Enforcement
  Program
Dept. of Social and
  Rehabilitation Services
2700 West Sixth
Topeka, KS 66606
(913) 296-3237

KENTUCKY
Division of Child Support
  Enforcement
Department of Social
  Insurance
Cabinet for Human Resources
275 East Main Street
Frankfort, KY 40621
(502) 564-2285

LOUISIANA
Support Enforcement
  Services Program
Office of Family Security
Department of Health and
  Human Resources
P.O. Box 94065
Baton Rouge, LA 70804
(504) 342-4780

MAINE
Support Enforcement and
  Location Unit
Bureau of Social Welfare
Department of Human Service
State House, Station 11
Augusta, ME 04333
(207) 289-2886

MARYLAND
Child Support Enforcement
  Administration
Department of Human
  Resources
11 East Mount Royal Avenue
Baltimore, MD 21201
(301) 333-3978

MASSACHUSETTS
Department of Revenue
Child Support Enforcement
  Division
215 First Street
Cambridge, MA 02142
(617) 621-4200

MICHIGAN
Office of Child Support
Department of Social
  Services

300 South Capital Avenue
Lansing, MI 48909
(517) 373-7570

MINNESOTA
Office of Child Support
Department of Human Ser-
  vices
Metro Square Building
St. Paul, MN 55101
(612) 296-2499

MISSISSIPPI
Child Support Division
State Department of Public
  Welfare
P.O. Box 352
515 East Amite Street
Jackson, MS 39205
(601) 354-0341, ext. 503

MISSOURI
Division of Child Support
  Enforcement
Department of Social
  Services
P.O. Box 1527
Jefferson City, MO 65102-1527
(314) 751-4301

MONTANA
Child Support Enforcement
  Program
Department of Revenue
Investigation and
  Enforcement Division
Helena, MT 59604
(406) 444-4614

NEBRASKA
Child Support Enforcement
  Office
Department of Social
  Services
P.O. Box 95026
Lincoln, NE 68509
(402) 271-9125

NEVADA
Child Support Enforcement
  Program
Department of Human
  Resources
2527 North Carson Street,
  Capitol Complex
Carson City, NV 89710
(702) 687-4239

NEW HAMPSHIRE
Office of Child Support
  Enforcement Services
Division of Welfare
Health and Welfare
  Building
Hazen Drive
Concord, NH 03301
(603) 271-4426

NEW JERSEY
Child Support and Paternity
  Unit
Department of Human
  Services
CN 716
Trenton, NJ 08625
(609) 538-2401

NEW MEXICO
Child Support Enforcement
  Bureau
Department of Human
  Services
P.O. Box 2348-PERA
Sante Fe, NM 87503
(505) 827-4230

NEW YORK
Office of Child Support
  Enforcement
New York State Dept. of Social
  Services
P.O. Box 14
1 Commerce Plaza
Albany, NY 12260
(518) 474-9081

NORTH CAROLINA
Child Support Enforcement
  Section
Division of Social Services
Department of Human
  Services
433 North Harrington street
Raleigh, NC 27603-1393
(919) 733-3582

NORTH DAKOTA
Child Support Enforcement
  Agency
North Dakota Dept. of Human
  Services
State Capitol
Bismarck, ND 58505
(701) 224-3582

OHIO
Bureau of Child Support
Ohio Department of Human
  Services
30 East Broad Street
Columbus, OH 43266-0423
(614) 466-3233

OKLAHOMA
Child Support Enforcement
  Unit
Department of Human
  Services
P.O. Box 25352
Oklahoma City, OK
  73125
(405) 424-5871

OREGON
Recovery Services Station
Adult and Family Services
  Division
Department of Human
  Resources
P.O. Box 14506
Salem, OR 97309
(503) 378-5439

PENNSYLVANIA
Bureau of Child Support
  Enforcement
Department of Public
  Welfare
P.O. Box 8018
Harrisburg, PA 17105
(717) 787-3672

PUERTO RICO
Child Support Enforcement
  Program
Department of Social Services
Call Box 3349
San Juan, PR 00904
(809) 722-4731

RHODE ISLAND
Bureau of Family Support
Department of Human
  Services
77 Dorrance Street
Providence, RI 02903
(401) 277-2409

SOUTH CAROLINA
Child Support Enforcement
  Division
Department of Social
  Services
P.O. Box 1520
Columbia, SC 29202-9988
(803) 737-9938

SOUTH DAKOTA
Office of Child Support
  Enforcement
Department of Social
  Services
700 Governors Drive
Pierre, SD 57501-2291
(605) 773-3641

TENNESSEE
Child Support Services
Department of Human
  Services

400 Deadrick Street
Nashville, TN 37219
(615) 741-1820

TEXAS
Child Support Enforcement
 Division
Office of Attorney General
P.O. Box 12548
Austin, TX 79711-2548
(512) 463-2181

UTAH
Office of Recovery Service
Department of Social
 Services
120 North 200 West
P.O. Box 45011
Salt Lake City, UT 84145-
 0011
(801) 538-4402

VERMONT
Child Support Division
Department of Social
 Welfare
103 South Main Street
Waterbury, VT 05676
(802) 241-2868

VIRGIN ISLANDS
Support and Paternity
 Division
Department of Law
46 Norre Gade
St. Thomas, VI 00801
(809) 776-0372

VIRGINIA
Division of Support
 Enforcement
Department of Social
 Services
8004 Franklin Farms Drive
Richmond, VA 23288
(804) 662-9297

WASHINGTON
Revenue Division
Department of Social and
 Health Services
P.O. Box 9162, Mail Stop
 PI-11
Olympia, WA 98504
(206) 459-6488

WEST VIRGINIA
Office of Child Support
 Enforcement
Department of Human
 Services
1900 Washington Street,
 East
Charleston, WV 25305
(304) 348-3780

WISCONSIN
Division of Community
 Services
Office of Child Support
1 West Wilson Street
P.O. Box 7851
Madison WI 53707-7851
(608) 266-1175

WYOMING
Child Support Enforcement
   Section
Div. of Public Assistance and
   Social Services

State Dept. of Health and
   Social Services
Hathaway Building
Cheyenne, WY 82002
(307) 777-789

CHAPTER ◇ 5

When a Parent Dies

We fear death. We avoid it. To talk about death is
not easy; it doesn't seem right. Death brings
with it a sense of "no tomorrow" that is almost
impossible to understand. Today one of every twenty children will face the death of a person close to them. That
means that in your classroom at school two or three of
your classmates will experience or already have experienced the death of someone they love. Like many people,
you probably first experienced death through a loss of a
pet. But you probably did not discuss the death.

Death is a taboo topic in most homes. You learn more
about death through what is not said about it than what
is. Robin remembers her pet cat. She came home from
school one day and went to her room. The cat wasn't on
the bed, its favorite place for an afternoon nap. Her
mother said the cat had "gone away." Robin was seven and
thought that meant the cat was hiding. She looked all over
the apartment but never found her. A few months later
her older brother told her the cat had died. The death of
Robin's pet was an "invisible" happening—here today,
gone tomorrow. Why had it died? What did it look like
dead? What did they do with her dead pet?

Robin has come face to face with death but not learned anything about it. Her mother tiptoed around the touchy subject instead of taking the opportunity to explain it. Even at age seven Robin could learn that death is a natural event. But parents should not be blamed if they avoid teaching their children about death. Our everyday world treats it as a taboo subject. There is almost no honest, sensitive treatment of death in American culture. It is a subject that is almost always shunned or trivialized.

What about television? Ninety-eight percent of American households with children own at least one television set. Young children spend more than four hours each day (and more on weekends) watching cartoons and TV shows. One source claims that 70 percent of the leading characters in action programs are involved in violence and death. There are six times as many violent episodes in one hour of children's cartoons as in one hour of adult programs. Television provides a mixed-up view of death. Seldom does anyone die naturally. In fact, in cartoons they rarely die at all! When death occurs it's "in a story," not really happening. Switch on the next TV program. What notion of the nature of death and dying can you learn from such exposure?

American society has changed. Until the 1950s, illness and death occurred mostly in the home, an experience shared by all family members. Children took an active part in, or at least watched, the funeral and the activities afterward. The impact of death was personal. The pain was shared. Death was not an unknown. In contrast, today's society has hospitals, hospices, nursing homes, and funeral homes. All the events associated with the dying and death of our loved ones are removed and distant. So we are left with the attitudes and information gained from the media and the accidental learning that occurs with our families and friends. We know very little about how we feel about death, or how we should feel, or what to do when a loved one dies.

If one of your parents has died, you may be painfully aware of the veil we throw over death. You are probably wondering why things have to be the way they are. This chapter will help you begin to untangle your feelings. Your parent's death might have been an unexpected shock. Perhaps your parent was ill and the death was expected. Whatever the cause, the loss of your parent is one of the most serious traumas you will ever experience. You will eventually move on, but right now you need to do something we are not very good at doing—think about death.

THINKING ABOUT DEATH

How you think about death will depend to a large degree on how you have been "programmed" (the attitudes you have learned and experiences you have had). Psychologists tell us that the idea of death goes through stages related to a child's age and level of mental development. Each stage is like a page in a coloring book. The colors you use on that page depend on how you've been "programmed," but the picture remains the same. Let's look at the different stages in life and how a child approaches death during the progression from infancy to adolescence. We have provided examples of what young people have said at different ages to give you a better understanding of their views of death.

Stage One: (Infancy to three)
- These children are too young to understand death consciously. They may react to the changes in their

lives by crying, throwing tantrums, or by turning inward and not reacting to people. They can become very depressed if they were especially attached to the parent. However, most infants' feelings are centered around their own needs, and if they are helped to feel secure, their emotions may not be very badly affected by the death of a parent.

Stage Two: (Early childhood—four through six)

• Death is not recognized as permanent. It's a "just-for-now" condition that can change. Researchers on death call this condition "reversible": A child knows that a person is no longer around, but this absence can be "reversed"; something has happened but something else will happen to make the person come back to life. Jimmy said the dead man was killed, but he "had to get up tomorrow."

• Children at this age typically engage in "magical thinking," make-believe, "I can make this happen." After the death of his baby brother, Ronny, five, told his mother, "I'm sorry, I didn't mean to do it." Ronny's brother had a birth defect and died at six months of age.

• Children also fear retaliation or feel guilt over their "bad" behavior that caused the death. Fears of monsters, bogeymen, and magical characters are also common.

Stage Three: (Middle childhood and preadolescence—seven through eleven)

• Death is understood as an irreversible event caused by murder, accident, or catastrophic event (volcano, hurricane, war). These events are external and happen to you.

• Toward the end of this stage, death is viewed as

more personal, caused by illness or old age, something that the child could not have stopped from happening.

- Children are really interested in the "gruesome" aspects of death. Kenny wanted to know what would happen if you were buried alive. Greg wanted to know how long it took a body to rot. Other questions: What happens at the undertaker's? Does a dead person's blood turn blue?
- Interest in the mystical, the hereafter, or voodoo aspects of death seems to become greater. June and her friends freaked out over vampire movies and wore crosses for several weeks. Jonathan, nine, lived close to a cemetery and told his friends the "living dead" came out at night.

Stage Four: (Adolescence—eleven through seventeen)

- Death is understood as irreversible and inevitable, something that happens to all of us.
- Death is a reality. A great deal of anxiety about death arises at this time.
- The awareness that death is a reality inevitably results in a kind of distancing that moves it into the future, thus reducing the threat. One teenager said, "I don't think about it much. I'm pretty healthy and have a lot of things to do, so I'll worry about it when I'm older."
- Religious beliefs are frequently relied upon as comfort. Reincarnation, heaven/hell, and life after death are topics of interest.

We have listed the stages to help you think about death in a real way. You may have a younger brother or sister in one of the stages. You may be able to read about feelings kids have at that stage and help your sibling understand more about your parent's death. Matthew's younger brother Rod had nightmares and had to sleep with the light on after the death of their mother. At age five he thought dead people lived in the dark; he remembered the preacher talking about "going forth from the darkness of death into the light." Lana's twin sister Lori became very religious after the death of their father. Lana couldn't understand it because they had never gone to church. Lori said she got a lot of comfort thinking about her father being in heaven, at peace and waiting for them.

You may not be able to understand other people's feelings about death. Their coloring book may look quite different from yours, and they may not understand yours. You may not understand your own feelings. Understanding some of these behaviors is a good place to start. In each stage of growing up, a person experiences real emotions, even though they may seem different to you. Matthew thought his brother was acting like a baby, being afraid of the dark. In Rod's mind, his behavior was protecting him from his fears; it was pretty normal behavior for someone his age. Going through the stages we have discussed is a natural part of growing up.

THE GRIEVING PROCESS

You might find it helpful to examine some of the emotions you felt after the death of your parent. You need to understand what sort of fears, fantasies, and misunderstandings you have collected along the way. Try talking to someone with whom you feel comfortable. Friends might help, but sometimes not; talking about death might make them feel strange and uncomfortable, especially if no one close to them has died. Talking it over with another family member or someone close, such as another relative or even a school counselor, is a good idea. Talking about your feelings helps you to understand and cope with them.

Whenever death is mentioned, you usually hear the word *grief*. Grief describes the feelings and behaviors of people at the death of someone close—friend, parent, or relative. It describes all of a person's reactions to a loss through death.

The Avoidance Phase

The reactions to grief begin with the *avoidance phase*. Shock and denial ("I can't believe this is happening") are felt by everyone. At this time the inability to believe what has happened (the denial) is good, because it allows you to absorb the reality of the loss a little at a time, rather than being completely overwhelmed. During this time you may feel confused, dazed, unable to concentrate or make decisions. Gradually things seem to clear up as you begin to accept the reality of a death.

The Confrontation Phase

As the reality continues to sink in, the second phase begins, the phase of *confrontation*. Feelings of anger, rage, envy, and resentment ("How could everyone let this happen?") are common as you begin to deal with your loss. Many times anger is directed at other people, frequently without any reason. Bitter feelings may be directed against God, the doctor, or yourself. Knowing that this behavior and these feelings are "not like you" is even more disturbing. Extremes of emotions are felt, and you seem to have no control.

Sonja, a thirteen-year-old, confessed that she hated her best friend for months after her mother died. "It just isn't fair that my friend's mother is still alive!" Mike found himself crying in the locker room after football practice. His teammates just stared, not knowing what to do. Mike said that all of a sudden it hit him that his father wouldn't be coming to any more games, and he just couldn't stop crying although he hated himself for acting like a baby. In this stage it is hard to predict what will set you off or how you will react. These "grief attacks" are scary but gradually go away. They are also natural, a perfect way of healing. Try to go with the flow of these feelings. Just let them happen and don't feel you have to explain them to others. Keeping the feelings bottled up will only make things worse.

A natural response to loss is always thinking about the person who died. You remember what they wore, how they smiled, the things they liked. Monica gathered up all her dead mother's perfume bottles and kept them in her room. Jess kept his dad's baseball caps and never missed a game on TV, especially when one of his dad's favorite teams was playing. He kept the scores and newspaper clippings just as he had done when his dad was alive.

This kind of behavior and collecting things to remind you of the dead person is also a natural way to help you feel less sad. It's a little like hugging someone and holding him close when saying good-bye. As you continue to do things you did before your parent died, you're helping yourself to accept the death and working toward the day when you can really "let go" of the dead person, really know that he or she is dead and gone forever from your life.

The Reestablishment Phase

The last phase of the grieving cycle is the *reestablishment phase*. Your grief gradually goes away and you are better able to cope. The loss is not forgotten, merely put away in a special place where it can be remembered. Now it is time to put your emotional energy into meeting new people, doing new and different things. Doing this marks the beginning of your return into the everyday world. Greg was surprised when he suddenly realized he was enjoying the movie he had gone to see with his friends. It was a war story, and he thought, "Dad would have liked this." Somehow, this time the thought did not make him quite so sad. Jess forgot to watch the Wednesday night baseball game; he was outside with his buddies. One reaction here is guilt over not remembering everything about your parent, over having fun, over "getting on with things." Like other feelings and behaviors you have learned to deal with, feelings of guilt are okay, but don't let them hang on forever. Remember, a time comes when you must get on with your own life while still holding fond memories of the person who died.

YOUR RELATIONS WITH FRIENDS

What are some reactions to others during a period of grieving? After reading thus far and looking back on your own experiences, you can probably figure out a few. Withdrawal is common and is particularly painful because it comes at a time when you need all the emotional and social support you can get. Other members of your family are going through the same things you are but may be so wrapped up in their own grief that they are unable to help. Many teenagers tell us that their friends cannot understand their feelings, and most don't want to talk about it. Death is scary. Having a friend who has lost a parent reminds them that it could happen to them too. At first they may avoid you or say or do things that make you feel hurt or angry.

Litecia suddenly felt grown up, older, and the things her friends did—like listening to music and talking about boys—seemed pretty babyish. She also felt guilty doing fun things so soon after her mother had died of cancer. That meant she spent a lot of time by herself, and loneliness made her more depressed.

Randy just didn't want to be around people. He felt restless and didn't know what he wanted to do. "It's as if the death of your parent puts up a barrier between you and other people. You don't know how, or are not willing to try, to get over the loss right now." Being unable or not wanting to get over a death is okay for a while, but try not to let these moods last too long. Look for help before you lose friends and get stuck in depression.

Give yourself time to heal. The death of a parent has made you a different person in many ways. You need time to understand your feelings and learn to handle them. Being with people will not be easy, and your social relationships will change. You may feel shy, afraid to love again, angry over your loss, and frightened by all these changes. Above all, try to share your feelings. Help may come from an unexpected source. You may have to look hard to find the person who can really help. Family members are good choices to start with. But, above all, keep looking.

YOUR BODY'S REACTION

The mind and body work together. When your body is sick, you "feel" sick. Many physical reactions come with emotional reactions to a loss. You may be surprised at how many people have these bodily reactions at the time of or after the death of a parent:

- Loss of appetite and weight
- Stomach upset
- Inability to sleep
- Tendency to sigh
- Lack of strength and a feeling of exhaustion
- Lack of energy
- Feeling of emptiness and heaviness throughout the body
- Feeling of "something stuck in my throat"
- Heart palpitations, shortness of breath, or both
- Nervousness and tension
- Loss of sexual desire or increased interest in sex
- Restlessness and constant searching for something to do

All these symptoms tell you that your body is still reacting to your grief. Gradually, as grief disappears and your life begins to return to normal once again, these reactions should go away. If they don't, you should see a doctor. But give yourself some time—healing doesn't come overnight.

WHEN TO GET EXTRA HELP

It should be pretty clear by now that dealing with the death of a parent is highly traumatic. It requires all your psychological and physical energy to do so in a healthy fashion. All the feelings you experience in the cycle of grief are part of the healing process. They help you accept the reality of the loss, experience the pain, and adjust to a world without the deceased. As you heal, you will be able to withdraw emotional energy in order to invest it in another relationship. In exploring your feelings, you may find that you accomplish quite a lot.

Sometimes you may feel a need for help. Things aren't working. You may see that the behaviors of your other parent or brother or sister aren't "right." It's pretty difficult to decide whether you or a family member needs assistance in working through grief, but some guidelines might help. A single symptom (unless it is very severe) is not significant, but observing a number of the following symptoms may tell you that additional help would be wise (Segal, 1989):

- Anxiety about further loss and preoccupation with dying
- Desire for reunion so strong as to cause a wish to die
- Apathy and depression
- Loss of self-esteem
- Exaggerated clinging to the surviving parent
- Absorption in daydreaming and inability to function in school
- New patterns of hyperactive, aggressive, or destructive behavior
- Stealing or other antisocial behavior that succeeds in gaining attention

When several of these behaviors form a pattern and persist, they interfere with day-to-day life. Then it is time for help. Your doctor, school counselor, or a family friend may be able to help you find a mental-health professional.

WILLIE'S STORY

After Willie's mother died he went to live with his aunt. In seventh grade Willie had gotten mostly Bs and Cs, but this year he was failing most of his subjects. He began swearing and getting in fights at school and seemed not to have any friends. He wouldn't mind his aunt, and he talked back to his teachers.

The school principal met with the aunt, Willie, and a school counselor, but Willie didn't like the counselor, so his aunt consulted their preacher. The preacher recognized Willie's need for help and got him involved in a church youth group. The young people played basketball, and after the games they sat and talked about different things. As the group began to plan a weekend activity, the group leader asked the kids to volunteer their parents. Willie suddenly began to cry.

His grief attack came eight long months after his mother's death. He had been unable to work out his feelings of anger and despair; instead, he had gotten stuck in a pattern of bad behavior and didn't know how to break it.

Willie got the help he needed to release his emotions and begin to heal. If he hadn't, he might have been caught in a bad downward spiral. In another year, he might have gotten into drugs as a way to stop the pain he felt and couldn't express. When feelings caused by the death of a parent are not expressed, they have a way of becoming twisted and negative.

The twisted feelings can last for months, even for years. They could prevent you from leading a full, active life. Now, not later, is the best time to deal with your experience of the loss of your parent.

DELAYED REACTIONS

You may be a teenager whose parent died a long time ago. Your family might have thought you were too young to understand the death and tried to shield you. Even if they tried to explain the death, you may still have unresolved feelings. You may wonder what your life would be like if your parent had lived. Some teenagers idealize the parents they have lost. Anger at their absence sometimes lingers. The anger is not bad; it shows how much they need their parent. You can't get angry about something unless you care. If you are a teenager dealing with the death of a parent that happened a long time ago, you should take the process very seriously. Discuss it with someone you trust or write your thoughts and feelings in a journal. You may find the following questions helpful.

1. How was the subject of death treated in your home when you were a child? What questions did you ask of your parent? What answers did you receive?
2. What most interested or puzzled you about death when you were a young child?
3. Do you remember the death of a pet or other animal at some time in your childhood? What were the circumstances? How did you feel about it? How did other people respond to your feelings?

4. Do you remember the death of your parent? What were the circumstances? How did you feel about it? How did other people respond to your feelings?
5. Can you identify any ways in which childhood experiences with death may have influenced you to this day?
6. What do you now think is the best thing a parent could say to or do with a child in a death situation, and why?
7. What do you now think is the worst thing a parent could say to or do with a child in a death situation, and why?

Living through the death of a parent teaches you many things. Most teenagers report that the experience drew their families closer. However, some families go through a tense, difficult period. One person may deal with his or her grief by withdrawing. Another might want to plan a memorial service where the family shares memories of the parent who has died. The person who has withdrawn might make his relatives angry by refusing to go to the memorial service.

You may find that you and your surviving parent don't agree about your behavior. They might try to "protect" you from the death and tell you not to attend the funeral though you want to go. Or, they may try to force you to grieve in a way that makes you uncomfortable. They might think only tears and silence are appropriate. You prefer to concentrate on remembering the good times you and your other parent had together.

Conflict sometimes breaks out in the time following the funeral. Your surviving parent may expect you to join him or her in mourning your dead parent. He or she may disapprove if you go to a party or dance. This is under-standable. Most religions once required a period of mourning. People wore special clothes and refrained from social activity. But times have changed. Grieving can be what you think is best for the situation. If you and your parent don't agree, pay close attention to the list of suggestions printed below. They were prepared by high school students in a support group. They are addressed to parents and explain what teenagers feel and need after the death of a parent.

1. Don't protect us. Let us know what is going on and how you feel. If we can see you cry, we'll feel free to cry ourselves. We need to feel that we belong and to share our feelings with you.

2. Don't make us feel guilty. Help us not to blame ourselves. Sometimes we don't realize that we are not to blame for the death. Adults need to tell us that; then we can deal with it.

3. Let us show grief our *own* way. You may want to cry; I may want to walk on the beach or read a book. Maybe I don't suffer out loud; let that be okay with you.

4. Help us feel secure. Don't force us to make too many changes in our lives. Death has been enough of a change. Familiar things and family customs help us keep our balance.

5. Be there for us. Don't give up on us. Sometimes we don't know why we do things. We're sure to learn as we grow up, but we need your help with the growing.

6. Let us help each other. Giving something back makes us feel loved and important. Help us to share our help with one another. Help us find out

our different needs; that way we can help each other a lot more.

Much of life is about beginnings and endings. Everyone knows deep down that death is a part of life, but few care to think about it. Living our lives is learning what lies between birth and death. If someone close to you has died, do all you can to make your parents talk to you about it, answer your questions, understand your grief, and help you get back to a normal guilt-free, grief-free daily life. You often hear people say, "You know, life goes on." That may sound pretty awful when you're feeling sad about a death, but it is true. Death or not, life does go on for you.

CHAPTER 6

Illness

The illness of a parent can be a major trauma. If you live in a single-parent home, you may find yourself on your own, facing new responsibilities. If you live in a two-parent family, one of your parents may be incapacitated. All of sudden, you may find yourself living in a type of single-parent household, even though both your parents are alive and married. Illness is confusing. It can be sudden or it can be expected. It will force you to reevaluate your family situation, and your place in it.

When Cindy came home from school one afternoon, her grandparents were waiting. They told her that her father was in the hospital with "heart problems" and her mother was with him. Just the look on their faces scared Cindy. Even though they said everything was all right, she did not believe them. They looked too scared to be reassuring. Cindy has never forgotten that moment, their faces, or the dramatic changes that took place in her life from that day on. Her father had suffered a stoke, and although Cindy did not know it that afternoon, he would not die. He would be sick for a long, long time—and her life would be changed forever.

Statistics are few on how many families in America have one parent who has a significant health problem. Many diseases (cancer, heart disease, lung disease, diabetes) as well as accidents and injuries can come into your life with an unexpected thud. If you live in such a family, the whole family needs to make some changes to cope with the sick parent. That can be quite a challenge but one that you may find easier to face if you have some information. You may also find help in learning from other teenagers who have found themselves in the same situation.

STAGES OF A PARENT'S ILLNESS

Finding Out

Dealing with a family illness comes in stages. The first stage is *finding out*. Sometimes finding out that your parent is sick comes gradually, just sort of creeps up on you. Other times, like Cindy, you find out with no warning. Either way, at first the finding out brings various emotions: shock, fear, helplessness, even anger and guilt. All these feelings are normal and a natural reaction. One thing that happens when you get bad news is that the message just doesn't sink in. Cindy couldn't believe it. She was frightened, and questions ran through her mind: "Why did it happen?" "Will he die?" "Who's going to take care of me?" She was scared and couldn't think straight.

Jerry's dad was in a car accident. Jerry was called out of school and went to the hospital with his mother. Sitting in the waiting room, he felt angry and betrayed. Dad was supposed to buy him a new baseball glove this week, and he needed that glove for the big game. Dad always took care of things like that. Now what? Almost at once Jerry felt guilty for thinking of himself instead of Dad. He couldn't believe this was happening to him. Not Dad!

Everyone reacts differently in shock. You don't know how to react, and most likely the people around you don't either. There is much confusion. It may be helpful to you to know that these feelings, as well as many you can't even describe, are natural and normal reactions to hearing news that is unexpected, upsetting. When children learn of a parent's illness, a question immediately pops into their mind: "What about me?" You're worried about your future. Deep down you've always been sure that your parents would always be around to take care of you. Even though you know they're not perfect, you still need to know you can count on them to look after everything. It's a shock to come face to face with the fact that maybe you can't count on that anymore. Cindy reacted with fear; Jerry reacted with anger. Most children say that shortly after learning about a parent's health problem their first thought is: "What's going to happen to me, to us?"

Jerry felt guilty about those feelings, but he shouldn't have. It's natural to want to feel secure. In fact, admitting to yourself that things have changed is healthy. Playing ostrich and keeping your head in the sand won't help you face reality. The very fact that you're worried about your security and future will help you deal with your parent's illness.

At first, everyone around you is trying to figure out what to do and how to act. The people around you change: Some try to make you feel better but end up making you feel worse. Megan said her relatives kept telling her: "Now dear, keep your chin up," and "You need to be strong for your mother, dear." Megan didn't feel like being strong! Her father had cancer, her younger sister was always crying, her mother was always at the hospital.

Megan felt afraid and alone. The more she tried not to cry or get upset, the worse she felt. One day a neighbor came over and asked, "Megan, how're you doing? I'm not doing so well; I think I need a good cry. How about you?" And Megan began to cry. It was such a relief to have someone with whom to share her feelings and not always have to act strong. She learned a good lesson: Help can come from unexpected sources.

Taking Some Action

If you feel alone and helpless you may need to take action. The first step in dealing with a parent's health problem is to let people know how you feel. Don't keep your feelings bottled up! Taking this kind of action will let others know you're trying to deal with your feelings in an honest manner. You need someone to talk to, someone with whom you can be yourself. Like Megan, you may find that person is a relative, teacher, friend, or someone you hadn't even dreamed could help you.

When things become uncomfortable, try to remember that everyone is uptight. Some may react by being angry and always grumpy; some may try to keep a stiff upper lip; others may give in to being sad and gloomy. Trying to figure out how anyone else will react can be hard. One good key is to try to recall how that person reacted in other tough situations. Jeff remembered that his grandmother did nothing but clean, wash dishes, and keep busy the last time his grandfather was sick. She didn't cry or seem upset, but she was always busy working and didn't want to talk. Karen's Aunt Babe cried at the drop of a hat and was always upset. Remembering how people have reacted in the past may give you some clues as to the way they act now. But don't spend much time trying to figure that out. Everyone needs to show a lot of patience toward one another. Sharing your feelings, either by talking about them or showing them, is a healthy way to feel better in a not-so-hot situation.

UNDERSTANDING YOUR ILL PARENT

Let's talk about your sick parent. Try to understand how he or she is feeling. A sick parent can have any or all of these feelings:

- Shock and denial: "I can't believe it! This can't be happening to me!"
- Panic: "I'm going to die for sure!"
- Helplessness: "I can't do a thing for myself!"
- Confusion: "I just don't understand any of this!"
- Inadequacy: "Now I'm good for absolutely nothing!"

Reactions Vary

Cliff's dad refused to believe that he might lose the use of his leg; he was mean and angry with everyone around him. He kept saying that if he could just get out of the hospital, he could take care of the leg himself. He was experiencing shock and denial. Ian's father couldn't stop talking about how he had to get out of the hospital in time to finish a business deal. No one else could do that job. He had to be there! This was panic over not being able to control his activities. Marta's stepmother had always been organized and independent. Now she wouldn't make any decision without "checking with the doctor." She couldn't stop talking about her operation and her medications. She needed help in making even the smallest decision. If you think about the ways you have seen your parent act, you can probably see that he or she fits with one of the above reactions or come up with a few of your own.

Sometimes an illness can just plain take over a parent, especially at first. The parent can't cope with the illness and all the feelings that go with it. Fran's mother became so withdrawn that she hardly paid any attention to the kids.

Hopefully, the doctors and nurses will understand and pay attention to your parent's behavior. At some point, however, you may feel that it is getting out of hand. Just as your parent needs help with the physical symptoms of the illness, he or she may need help dealing with it emotionally. Discuss your concerns with your other parent, a relative, or the doctor. Don't be afraid to ask for help. The doctor, the nurse, or a counselor may also be able to give you advice on how to help your parent—but you need to seek this help.

Managing the Illness

Cindy heard the family doctor talking about her father's stroke. That was confusing because her grandparents kept referring to "it," and her mother called it a "heart problem." Nobody was very specific. Cindy couldn't understand how a heart problem would affect his speech and ability to use his right arm. She went to the library and looked up information on the heart, heart disease, and strokes. She took notes and made copies to take home. She left the copies on the kitchen table, hoping someone would notice them, and her mother did. Cindy told her mother that she was confused, afraid, and needed to know what was happening. Cindy's mother understood then that her daughter needed to be informed and involved, not protected. They studied and discussed the information together.

To get ready to deal with the health problem, you need to begin by getting information. One of the main road-blocks to that may be the people around you. Cindy's mother and her grandparents wanted to protect her by telling her very little about her father's condition. Cindy found that frightening and felt left out. Although you have to deal with the health problem, how much do you want to know? That is a personal decision. Like Cindy, you may be curious and think you'd feel better if you had more information. Megan did not want to know. She found it frightening enough to go to the hospital and needed more time to deal with her father's cancer. Think about it—illness can be frightening. There are no defi-nite answers. Sometimes there are not even "truthful" answers, because the answers are not known. Megan knew that her father was undergoing chemotherapy. The doctors were not sure it would cure the cancer, but they had to try. Most of us think either doctors or me-dicine will make us well again; sometimes that is not the case. Doctors and medicine can help but not always cure. Knowing as much as you can about your parent's health problem will help you cope, but how much infor-mation you want or think you can handle also needs to be considered.

You need information about

- the disease or injury (exactly what is the problem?);
- the treatment (what kind of treatment(s) is your parent to receive?); and
- the medicines your parent is taking (what are they?).

DAN'S STORY

When Dan's father was released from the hospital after back surgery, he had to lie flat on his back in bed for six weeks. He was often so groggy and "out of it" that Dan gradually stopped going into his room. Dan was disgusted by the way his dad looked, and what's more, he had to use a catheter. One day his dad yelled for Dan to come help him. Dan, although he was sixteen, hid in his room and refused to come out. Later that evening he heard his father crying. Dan was frightened; he had never seen or heard him cry. He heard his father talking: "I hate being like this, like a baby," and "Everyone thinks I'm a burden."

Later that evening Dan phoned his aunt and learned quite a few things. The pain medication made his dad groggy; the colostomy bag with the catheter was necessary because of swelling and muscle paralysis; his dad was becoming severely depressed because of lack of activity and the family's avoidance of him. How come no one had told Dan all this? Why hadn't he asked? It really wasn't anyone's fault, but everyone had to share the blame. Knowing more about the surgery, what would happen during his dad's recuperation, and the effects of his medication would have enabled Dan to understand all the things he found disgusting. Knowing sooner would have made him a little more patient and more willing to help.

Where can you get the information? Make your own list of questions. Your grandparent or anyone else familiar with your parent's health problem can be of help. Write down the name of the health problem/disease/injury, the name of the medication, and the name/description of the treatment. Knowing what caused the problem may help you understand the treatment. Many medications and treatments may be recommended for one health problem. You will need help in relating all this to your parent's particular case. Remember, every person is different.

A side note: Finding out about your parent's health problem may help you answer other questions that may have been lurking in your mind. Most children are concerned that they may have caused the parent's health problems or will "get" the same disease. You don't have the power to make your parent sick. There are always many reasons for a particular illness, and none is the fault of a child. It is natural to feel a little guilty, but you must use common sense before "blaming" anyone, especially yourself.

CHANGES IN YOUR LIFE

Educating yourself about your parent's health problem is just one more challenge you face. The situation may also bring about changes in your life:

- Finances (less money to spend)
- Social relationships (fewer friends)
- Activities (less time to do things you like).

Some health problems last only a short time, even though they can be quite serious. Dan's father was in bed for several months before things gradually improved. Although "short-term" health problems may involve hospitalization or surgery, they won't last forever. Some health problems last a long time, however. Long-term illness may be far harder to get used to and may bring about far more family changes.

Regardless of the length of the illness, getting sick is an expensive business. Medical insurance may pay part of the bills, but rarely all. Your family will have to plan for the shortage and work together to make ends meet. Some teenagers resent all the money spent on their parent's illness and the lack of money for themselves. Sound like a natural reaction? It is. But having less money may be a fact and will not be remedied by complaining about it. How do you think your ill parent feels? Most seriously ill people feel constantly stressed and guilty over how much their treatment costs; yet they cannot do anything about it. Try to help out. Find ways to save or earn money. You'll feel as if you're contributing and regaining some control over your life.

Your Social Life

How will your social life change? Mandy had to take over more of the household chores while her mother was in the hospital. Her older brother had to work, and that left her younger brother and sister at home after school and on weekends. Mandy was twelve and more than able to care for them, but her responsibilities left less time for her friends.

Maria found herself alone, at loose ends. Her grandmother was always at the hospital with her mother, leaving Maria to take care of herself. Maria was seventeen and often had thought she would give anything to have the house to herself. But now that everyone was gone, she was lonely and afraid.

Not only will your social relationships change, but friends and relatives may play different roles in your life. Family friends may not be around as much since your parent is ill. They may spend more time with your ill parent. Relatives may try to take the place of your parent. Eleanor's Aunt Barbara moved in with them to help out until her mother got home. This "helping out" also turned into a lot of advice and orders. Eleanor didn't like being bossed around. She remembered when her aunt was fun, not always telling her what to do.

Your Activities

The kinds of activities in which you participate will hinge on your finances and your new responsibilities. Some new activities will creep in, like taking care of your sick parent or visiting the hospital. You'll want to save time for such visits. You may have fewer activities around the house if your parent is recuperating at home. Quiet activities may replace more active ones. Playing cards instead of football may become better recreation for your brothers and sisters. Meal schedules may be changed to meet the needs of your parent. Weekend trips, vacations, and family outings can be changed to include everyone. But your entire life does NOT have to change. You can easily plan more family-type activities so that your parent is not left out. The main goal is to keep some fun in your life, to be creative, and do interesting things. Katie learned to play canasta with her grandmother; when her mom felt well enough she would join them. Katie and her grandmother determined to learn one new game each week; this turned out to be more fun than Katie thought. Her mother also looked forward to the games; they eased her boredom and provided a fun way for Katie to be with her.

PARENT CARE

A decision has been made on whether to provide health care for your parent at home or in the hospital.

At Home

If your parent recuperates at home, it is a good idea to organize a family council and figure out who has what responsibilities. Someone may need to come to live with you: an aunt, uncle, friend, or nurse. For a while, your home may become a mini-hospital. Many of the things you do may have a medical flavor. Meals for your parent will probably be planned by the doctor, so your eating habits may change. Family members must know what and how much your parent can eat and drink. Medications have to be given, and you may find yourself helping out or in charge.

Helping with medication is a large responsibility and one you cannot take lightly. If you don't understand the prescription instructions, talk to the doctor or the pharmacist. *Don't stop asking questions until you understand.* When you do understand, be sure to follow the directions. Everyone knows this, or should, but it must be stated very clearly: *Keep all medications in a safe place*, away from children and, when necessary, from the patient. Keep a list of phone numbers handy: the hospital, the doctor's office, Aunt Babe's. Keeping things organized will help, especially if you're in a hurry or just plain frazzled.

Len's dad had always shot hoops with the boys. Now, because of multiple sclerosis, he was in a wheelchair and could barely raise his arms. This was not the dad Len knew or his friends could relate to! One of Len's friends came over one day to pick him up for a movie and saw Len's dad in the living room. Dave went directly over to him and said, "Hey, Mr. D! What's happening?" Len's dad said, "As you can see, I'm not playing any basketball, but I'm still Len's dad and your friend! Good to see you!"

Get the point? Illness had certainly changed his physical shell, but underneath he was still the man they had played basketball with. You have shared many good memories with your parent, and more will come. Try not to concentrate on the physical or emotional aspects of the illness that detract from what you have done together. True, Len will never again play basketball with his dad. In the past he had, and loved it, and he can remember that. Look for new things to share that can be accomplished within the limits of the illness. If having friends see your parent is hurtful, don't do it. Find other ways to stay involved with your friends—and your parent. Realize that during the course of your parent's illness you will feel resentful or angry. Feel it, then let it go. Make positive changes in your home environment, write them down, discuss them with your family, and try them out. What have you got to lose?

Remember to keep your parent involved! Perhaps Len's dad could help him with his math, or they could watch an NBA game together. One family got an idea from a magazine article called, "Notes from the Bedpost." Every night they went to their father's room with a "newspaper" full of schoolwork, newspaper articles, jokes, or pictures they had drawn. During the day they had to let him rest, but this half hour was their time together.

Expect good and bad days. Illness and medication often go in cycles. Your parent may feel better in the morning but terrible at night. Plan your activities around those feelings, if possible. Living with an illness can be stressful. Chapter 7 has information on dealing with stress. You may want to share some of the tips with family members. Offering a listening ear or a friendly smile on a particularly bad day is sure to be appreciated and may help you understand how they're feeling.

In the Hospital

Many people feel uncomfortable in hospitals. Visiting your parent in a hospital and getting used to the environment is a requirement during a serious illness. You'll need to find out about visiting hours, special rules, and what to expect when you get there.

If you have a strong reaction to visiting your parent in this setting, take it in small steps. Go for a few minutes to drop off a magazine or just to say hello. Work up to longer periods of time as you're able to handle them. Miriam hated hospital visits, but since her aunt worked and couldn't go in the evenings, she visited her mother then. She took things to do and made a list of things to talk about (neighborhood gossip, news, personal activities).

Knowing the kind of medical treatment your parent is undergoing may help you understand his or her appearance or behavior. Chris knew his father's face would be puffed up because of the medication. It was a shock at first but gradually became part of what he expected to see.

When your parent is in the hospital you have to abide by its rules. It may be more convenient for you to stop by after school, but that may be when nurses are giving baths or medication. Becoming familiar with the hospital routine and your parent's activities will help you plan your visiting time. Getting to know the nurses on duty or the doctor is a good idea. A good relationship with them makes everyone feel easier.

Changes in your parent's condition at the hospital can catch you off guard. If your parents is having a particularly difficult spell, it might be wise to call the hospital in advance. In that way, you can be prepared for any change in treatment, equipment, or your parent's physical appearance or behavior. That nurse you've come to know can be a big help in this instance.

TAKING CARE OF ME

When a parent becomes ill, family roles are often reversed. The person who always took care of you is the one needing care. Many teenagers save the day. They shoulder responsibility around the house and help the family stay together. Later in life, when they look back, they realize the crisis was a turning point. They got a taste of reality, learned new skills, and became more self-reliant. Bill, age eighteen and a freshman at college, put it this way: "When my mother had a breakdown and went to the hospital, I was fourteen. She stayed for six months. It was a really tough time, but my whole family is tougher now too. I iron my own shirts, do my own laundry, change the oil in the car. My little sister can fix a clogged drain. How about that?"

If you are coping with a sick parent, you too are at a turning point in your life. You're probably learning and doing more than you ever thought possible. But don't get swallowed up by your parent's illness. No matter how much you love them and want to help, you need to think about getting on with your life and taking care of your own health.

Keeping healthy mentally and physically is a big challenge in everyday life. It is especially important for you. Good health can equip you with enough strength to meet daily challenges. Throughout your parent's illness you have continued to learn new things, make new friends, and have new experiences. But it is important not to let your parent's illness control your life. You are an individual; that has not changed.

An organization called Cancer Care of Cincinnati has drawn up a Bill of Rights for families. Although it deals primarily with cancer, it can be applied toward any illness.

- I have the RIGHT to enjoy my own good health without feeling guilty. It's not my fault that someone I love has cancer.
- Even if only a child, I have a RIGHT to know what's going on in our family. I have a right to be told the truth about cancer in words I can understand.
- I do not always have to agree with someone just because that person has cancer.
- I can get angry at the person without always feeling guilty, because sickness does not stop someone from being a person.
- I have a RIGHT to feel what I feel—not what someone else says I "should" feel.
- I have a RIGHT to look after my own needs, even if they do not seem as great as the patient's. I am permitted to take "time out" from the cancer without feeling disloyal.
- I have a RIGHT to get outside help for the patient if I can't manage all the responsibilities of home care myself.

- I have the RIGHT to get help for myself, even if others in my family choose not to do so.

Handling the pressure of having an ill parent is a huge task—a task shared by everyone: your brothers and sisters and anyone who cares about your family. Like Bill, you need to take pride in the positive things you have accomplished and move on to more. It is easy to get sidetracked with so many things going on in your life. Many of those things may seem negative. Develop a list of goals, things *you* want to accomplish, and continue to work toward them. Write down things that help you handle the pressure: maybe working out when you get mad instead of yelling at someone, or hiding in a corner with a good book or magazine instead of stressing out. Learning how to deal with an illness takes time. Set goals, try to be positive, and take pride in what you have accomplished.

CHAPTER ◇ 7

Moving On

Being a teenager is never easy. One minute you are being talked down to, and the next you are given grown-up responsibilities. Adolescence is a rough time, and no matter how good your life is, it can often be hard to handle.

If you live in a single-parent home, your life just becomes that much more confusing. One of your parents is out of the picture. Often, the parent you live with will expect you to handle all the responsibilities created by a decision you had no part in making. This can be both flattering and frustrating.

Now that you're living in a single-parent home, your parent is treating you as an adult. You're given both more responsibility and more freedom. If you have younger sisters or brothers, you may find that your parent turns to you for advice on how to deal with them. Because of your age, you are expected to be able to take care of yourself while your parent copes with keeping the family together.

This, of course, further complicates your life. You are suddenly being treated as an adult, and you probably didn't realize exactly what that meant before it was thrust upon you. Your parent is no longer taking care of every little thing for you and making sure everything in your life runs smoothly; he or she has other things that must get done. You are now responsible for all kinds of things you took for granted.

This change in status can be very confusing. You are probably still dealing with the loss of your parent; now on top of that you have to do the dishes and perhaps get a part-time job. You may feel angry that you are expected to handle all this responsibility. After all, you aren't legally an adult; why should you have the responsibilities of one? You may also feel helpless and out of control. You are expected to be able to do things you're not quite sure you can do. You may feel lonely, thinking no one understands what you're going through. Your parent is probably extremely busy and does not have as much time for you as usual; your friends may not understand that you can't go to the movies because you can't afford it. If your parent has told you some of the problems and worries that have come up for her or for him, you may find yourself dwelling on them. You may be afraid of the future.

None of these feelings is bad or weak. These emotions are normal and expected. You have been catapulted into a situation for which you were unprepared. You are not expected to just dust yourself off and go with the flow. You just have to think through your feelings and talk them out. Don't deny them; that will only make you miserable. Don't become obsessed with them; they will take over your life if you let them. You have to accept that you have these feelings and learn how to deal with them so that you can take control of your life.

TAKING CONTROL OF YOUR LIFE

The first step in dealing with your problems is recognizing that the problems are there. That may sound silly or obvious, but in truth, sometimes it's easier to pretend you have no problems than it is to face up to them and try to solve them. Unfortunately, pretending the problems aren't there doesn't make them go away, and they can get much worse while you are ignoring them. You can't solve a problem if you don't admit it exists. No one's life is perfect, and everyone is entitled to a few imperfect emotions. Admitting them doesn't make you a weak or ungrateful person; it shows that you are mature and responsible enough to handle your life.

The next step is defining the problem. You've been feeling unhappy lately. If you don't know what's been causing your unhappiness you can't fix your problem. Sit down and think about where your feelings have been coming from. Talk them out with your parent or with someone you trust—sometimes you are too close to a problem to see it clearly. You might try writing down your feelings if you're not comfortable discussing them with anyone. Sometimes seeing everything on paper can produce startling revelations.

The next step is probably the hardest. Find solutions to the problem. Come up with a workable solution to whatever is bothering you. Once again, sometimes it can help to talk with someone; two heads are better than one, and someone else is likely to think of solutions you would never have considered. Once you have a possible solution, evaluate it; that is, think realistically about whether it can work. Get a good idea about what the results of that solution would be. Let yourself be comfortable with the idea.

Then, when you think you're ready, put your idea into practice.

YOUR COMMUNICATION SKILLS

There is one thing you can do that is likely to stop problems before they start. That is to communicate. Talk to your parent, your family, and your friends. Communication is one of the ways you can cut disagreement off at the pass. It makes no difference how shy or quiet a person you may be, or how much you hate talking about yourself and your feelings. If you don't learn to talk, discuss, express your ideas, or in other words, communicate, you won't get anywhere in solving your problems. Worse, you will have many more problems than you would if you had communicated with people.

Communication means that you have to listen and understand other people's feelings and ideas. How many fights have you had in your life over a simple misunderstanding? How many arguments during which you were both saying the same thing but were yelling too loud to hear that? If you talk about your feelings calmly, and even more important, listen to other people's feelings, they will most likely return the favor and you will avoid many pointless disagreements. Through good communication you can hear some of your own problems defined, maybe for the first time; often when you hear someone else's words on a subject, the problem takes on a whole new aspect, and suddenly a solution appears. People can help you better if you help them understand your feelings and problems. You owe it to yourself to make your life happier through good communication.

Here are some tips for good communication:

- Look at the person you're talking with, and make eye contact. This will help the person realize you are interested in his or her viewpoint, and that person will be likely to say more to you.
- Listen carefully to what is being said.
- Keep your mind on the conversation. If you let your attention drift, the person you are talking with will assume you don't care about the conversation.
- Speak so that the other person can understand you. Ask if you are making yourself clear. If not, find other words to explain what you have in mind. Otherwise you aren't communicating; you're just repeating yourself endlessly.
- Let the person know you understand what's being said, and that you care. When you nod, smile, or murmur "uh–huh" every so often, the other person feels you are paying attention. People need encouragement to keep talking.
- Be sure you're calm and have your thoughts together, and that you're really ready to speak. There is an old maxim, "Think before you speak." It can save a lot of misunderstanding and apologizing later if you choose your words well in the first place.
- Make sure that you and the other person are in the right mood both to talk and listen. If one of you is going to storm away at the least criticism, the effort will be a waste. Pick a time, together, that is good for both of you.
- Have your talk in a place where you won't be disturbed. There is nothing more frustrating than being interrupted in the middle of a serious conversation.

- Be patient. Don't let your emotions cause you to say and do things that you don't mean, and don't give up if the conversation isn't going the way you want it to within the first thirty seconds. Real understanding always takes time.

These suggestions can be surprisingly hard to follow, but *do* make the effort. It's worth it.

DEALING WITH STRESS

The odds are that you are very stressed out. You are a teenager, which is stressful enough. You are in a single-parent home, which can be exciting but at the same time is often draining. If you don't deal with stress and find ways to relax, you may find yourself angry and sad for reasons you can't even identify. Every time something happens that upsets you, no matter how small it is, deal with it, or you will become more stressed. Don't allow yourself to become that stressed out. When someone does something that annoys you, tell that person. Don't be rude about it, but don't ignore it either. Sometimes people don't realize what they are doing.

The more positive you feel and act in your life, the easier it will be to cope with your stress. If you don't let little things bother you, you won't get upset. Stress can have a pretty unbelievable effect on our lives if we let it get out of control. Researchers on stress have found it causes the following reactions or responses:

Physical Responses
Stomach problems
Headaches

Short or rapid breathing
Insomnia or other sleep disorders
Nausea
Diarrhea
Hives/skin rash
Muscle tightness

Emotional Responses
Depression; feeling down in the dumps
Restlessness
Crying for no reason
Moodiness
Unusual behavior patterns
Withdrawal from family and friends
Blaming others
Fear of promising anything to anyone
Feeling uptight in normal situations

Intellectual Responses
Inability to concentrate
Lack of enthusiasm to do things
Lack of interest in details
Preoccupation with negative or angry thoughts
Tendency to make silly errors
Inability to get things done
Forgetfulness
Low grades and loss of friends

Don't be afraid to tell your parent when you're too stressed out to cope with life. Ask for some time away from the house. Maybe you could spend the weekend at a friend's house. Your parent knows what being stressed out is like. He or she knows how hard it can be to cope with things.

* * *

Making the change to a single-parent household can be difficult. But once you settle into it, life will improve. The odds are you will have more responsibility and less free time. But you also will be growing up. You will become mature, capable, and strong. And in the end, you will have learned to cope with problems.

Glossary

adoption   When a minor is accepted into a family other than his or her birth family and given the same rights as a child born into the family.

alimony   Financial support paid by one ex-spouse to the other after a divorce; the court determines the amount and the number of payments.

alternating custody   When the divorce court decides a minor will live first with one parent and then the other; an example would be a minor who lives with his or her mother during the school year and his or her father during the summer.

apathy   Lack of concern or feeling for.

child support   Money that a divorced parent is required to pay to the custodial parent for care of their children; the divorce court determines the amount and timing of the payments.

confidential adoption   (also known as closed adoption) An adoption in which the birth parents and adoptive parents do not and cannot know one another; the adoptive family has full legal entitlement to the child until the age of eighteen.

custody   The legal right of a divorced parent to assume guardianship of children from his or her marriage; there are several types of custody agreements.

desertion   When one parent leaves his or her family without warning and fails to meet family responsibilities.

divorce   The legal arrangement that dissolves a marriage. It usually divides the family property and sets up a custody and support arrangement for the couple's children.

international adoption   The adoption of a child from a foreign country.

joint legal custody   The legal term for the shared child-rearing responsibilities, not including living arrangements, between divorced parents.

joint physical custody   The legal term for the shared child-rearing responsibilities, including living arrangements, between divorced parents.

open adoption   An adoption in which one or both the birth parents know the identity of the adoptive family and retain the right to have contact with the child.

separation   The decision by a married couple to live apart; if it is a legal separation, lawyers have drawn up a separation agreement and filed it in the state judicial system.

temporary custody order   A court order giving one parent legal custody of the child until the divorce is final.

temporary support order   A court order made during divorce proceedings that requires a parent continue to pay for family expenses.

temporary vacate order   A court order made during divorce proceedings that requires one parent to leave the home.

third-party custody   The court-appointed guardian, not one of the parents, for a child. He or she is usually a relative, family friend, or lawyer.

Where to Go for Help

Al-Anon/Family Group Headquarters
P.O. Box 862
Midtown Station
New York, NY 10018
(800) 344-2666

Big Brothers/Big Sisters of America
230 North 13th Street
Philadelphia, PA 19107
(215) 567-7000

Child Help/I.O.F. Forester's National Child Abuse Hotline
(800) 4-A-CHILD

Children of Lesbians and Gays Everywhere
Gay and Lesbian Parents Coalition, International
Box 50360
Washington, DC 20091
(202) 583-8029

Children's Rights Council
220 I Street NE, #230
Washington, DC 20002
(202) 547-6227

Family Resource Coalition
200 South Michigan Avenue
Suite 1520
Chicago, IL 60604
(312) 341-0900

International Youth Council of Parents without Partners
8807 Colesville Road
Silver Spring, MD 20910
(301) 588-9354

National Men's Resource Center
P.O. Box 800-PR
San Anselmo, CA 94979
(415) 453-2389

National Organization of Single Mothers
P.O. Box 68
Midland, NC 28107-0068
(704) 888-5063

National Rainbow Coalition
1700 K Street NW
Washington, DC 20006
(202) 728-1180

National Youth Crisis Hotline
(800) 662-HELP

Personal Counselors
719 Second Avenue North
Seattle, WA 98109
(206) 284-0311

Single Parents Resource Center
141 West 28th Street, Suite 302
New York, NY 10001
(212) 947-0221

The Fatherhood Project
c/o The Families and Work Institute
330 7th Avenue, 14th Floor
New York, NY 10001
(212) 268-4846

United Way, First Call for Help
Contact your local office for referrals to numerous support
    services.

YMCA/YWCA
Contact your local branch for support services.

For Further Reading

Alexander, Shoshana. *In Praise of Single Parents; Mothers and Fathers Embracing the Challenge*. Boston/NYC: Houghton Mifflin, 1994.

Communication. New York: Greenwillow, 1993.

Coontz, Stephanie. *The Way We Never Were: American Families and the Nostalgia Trap*. New York: Basic, 1992.

Eisenberg, Ronni, with Kate Kelly. *Organize Your Family! Simple Routines for You and Your Kids*. New York: Hyperion, 1993.

Feldman, Robert S. *Understanding Stress*. New York: Franklin Watts, 1992

Krementz, Jill. *How It Feels To Be Adopted*. New York: Alfred A. Knopf, 1996.

Lash, Michelle, Sally Ives Loughridge, and David Fassler. *My Kind of Family: A Book for Kids in Single-Parent Homes*. Burlington, VT: Waterfront Books, 1990.

LeShan, Eda. *Learning to Say Good-bye: When a Parent Dies*. New York: Avon Books, 1993.

Mattes, Jane. *Single Mothers by Choice*. New York: Times Books, 1994.

Packer, Alex J. *Bringing Up Parents: The Teenager's Handbook*. Minneapolis, MN: Free Spirit Publishing, 1992.

Pearson, Carol Lynn. *One on the Seesaw: The Ups and Downs of a Single-Parent Family*. New York: Random House, 1988.

Pellegrini, Nina. *Families Are Different*. New York: Holiday House, 1991.

Salk, Dr. Lee. *Familyhood: Nurturing the Values that Matter*. New York: Simon and Schuster, 1992.

Scull, Charles, ed. *Fathers, Sons, and Daughters: Exploring Fatherhood, Renewing the Bond.* Los Angeles: J.P. Tarcher, 1992.

Stephenson, June. *The Two-Parent Family Is Not the Best.* Napa, CA: Diemar, Smith Publishing Co., 1991.

Weston, Kath. *Families We Choose: Lesbians, Gays, Kinship.* New York: Columbia University Press, 1991.

Index